MURDER UNPROMPTED

MURDER UNPROMPTED

A Crime Novel

by

SIMON BRETT

toExcel
San Jose New York Lincoln Shanghai

Murder Unprompted

Published by toExcel
an imprint of iUniverse.com, Inc.

For information address:
iUniverse.com, Inc.
620 North 48th Street
Suite 201
Lincoln, NE 68504-3467
www.iuniverse.com

ISBN: 0-595-00355-9

Printed in the United States of America

To Dany, with love

CHAPTER ONE

CHARLES PARIS was in the Number One dressing room.

True, the Number One dressing room at the Prince's Theatre, Taunton was distinguished from the other dressing rooms only by the white plastic numeral screwed on to the door. In size and lack of amenities they were all identical.

And true, Charles was sharing the Number One dressing room with another actor, Alex Household, who had a larger part in the play.

But the fact remained that, for the duration of the three week run of *The Hooded Owl*, Charles Paris would be in the Number One dressing room and, though publicly he always affected disinterest in such petty distinctions ("Men are led by toys", he would say, loftily quoting Napoleon), he was secretly delighted. However cynical he appeared, however logical he was about the likelihood of a sudden breakthrough at the age of fifty-four, his actor's imagination could still leap in seconds to the pinnacles of theatrical success. Dreams of sudden public recognition of his talents had survived almost unchanged from his teens, and reality, in the form of modest achievements and much "resting" since he had started in the business in 1949, could make little impression on them.

So, though he would never actually speak of it, even in his most drunken moments (which in his case were *quite* drunken), Charles still nursed the tiny hope that *The Hooded Owl* would be the one, the play on whose crest he would ride into the West End, where his true worth would be instantly appreciated, and he would spend the rest of his life "reading scripts" rather than grabbing any job that came within reach, becoming a regular on television chat shows, participating in "Nights of a Thousand Stars" for charity, and describing his favourite room to the *Observer* Colour Supplement.

Since he lived in one room, a dingy bed-sit in Hereford Road, London W.2., this last part of the fantasy had not been fully thought through. In fact, none of it had been fully thought through, because, in small

7

measure, he had tasted success. He had been in long runs in the West End, he had even had his own play running in the West End, he had done bits in television and films, and his logical self knew how insubstantial such satisfactions were.

And yet the fantasies persisted. It was just as it had been in his teens. In the early years of adolescence, he had put down all his feelings of dissatisfaction to the fact that he hadn't got that all-important amulet, a girl-friend. But, to his surprise, at the age of nineteen, after a steady two-year relationship, he had found he was still attributing his discontent to the same cause. Like the horizon, a sense of fulfilment kept its distance, regardless of his position.

But, in spite of that bleak conclusion, hope survived.

Hope for the future of *The Hooded Owl* was not quite as baseless as it might be for the average production in a provincial theatre. The staple diet of Taunton's theatre-goers was set-book classics, creaking but well-built thrillers and last year's West End cast-offs, none of which had any prospects beyond the three weeks of their run. *The Hooded Owl*, on the other hand, was a new play, and not a bad one at that. If all of the thousands of variables which govern such a process came right, it was not impossible that the play should transfer to the West End.

One person believed that possibility with sufficient conviction to back his belief with money. His name was Paul Lexington, and he called himself a producer. He certainly had a letterhead on his note-paper to prove it, though details of his actual productions seemed a little less well-defined. He talked confidently of tours he had set up with Music Hall shows and even mentioned putting on a pantomime, though at what level these productions had been mounted, it was difficult to assess. A tour of a Music Hall show could be anything from a glamorous parade of the country's Number One provincial theatres down to a glorified pub-crawl, with a motley band of barnstormers passing the hat round after a few songs at the piano.

Since Charles Paris had not heard of any major Music Hall tour in the previous few years, he inclined to the opinion that the operations of Paul Lexington Productions had been at the more modest level. On the other hand, impresarios have to start somewhere, Paul Lexington seemed a pleasant and knowledgeable young man and, in a business peopled with the incompetent and the frankly criminal, Charles felt inclined to give him the benefit of the doubt.

After all, without Paul Lexington, he would not be currently employed, and, if there was one thing that Charles's experience in the theatre had taught him, it was the inestimable advantage of having a job over "resting".

The sequence of events which had brought *The Hooded Owl* to its first night at the Prince's Theatre, Taunton, had been that usual circuitous trip through an obstacle course by which new plays reach the stage. The work had been written by a schoolmaster called Malcolm Harris who, though of undoubted talent, had no contacts in or knowledge of commercial theatre. He had lavished three years of his spare time on the work and, when he had the final draft neatly typed up with a Letrasetted front page and a transparent plastic folder, the only person he could think to send it to was the Professor of English at the university he had left twelve years previously. The Professor, after a few months' delay and an apologetically nudging letter from the playwright, had written back in terms of vague praise, which a professional writer would have recognised as a confession of not having read the script, and said he had passed it on to the Professor who headed the university's recently-inaugurated Drama Department. This gentleman, after a few months' delay and an apologetically nudging letter from the playwright, had written back to say he had passed it on to an actor friend who was setting up a new fringe theatre company in Surbiton. After quite a few months' delay, and three apologetically nudging letters from the playwright, the actor scribbled a note back, from an address in Gloucestershire, saying he was sorry he hadn't yet had time to read the play. And also he was sorry that he seemed to have lost the manuscript. And, anyway, he had decided that the theatre wasn't for him after all and he'd set up an antique shop with a friend.

Phase One of the offensive was thus over, and Phase Two started with the top carbon of the play, a newly-Letrasetted front page and a new transparent plastic folder. This time, on the advice of his wife's mother, who'd just read a biography of some playwright out of the library though she couldn't remember what his name was, Malcolm Harris had sent the play to his local repertory theatre. After a few months' delay and an apologetically nudging letter from the playwright, the General Manager had returned the script with a duplicated letter, saying thanks very much for sending it, the Play Selection Committee had found it really interesting, but unfortunately it wasn't the sort of show they were looking for at that time, why not try sending it to an agent? This Malcolm Harris had done, but, unfortunately, due to the random selection method of sticking a pin in the "Theatrical and Variety Agents" section

9

of the Yellow Pages, he had sent it to one who specialised in booking blue comedians and strippers into Working Men's Clubs. After a few months' delay and an apologetically nudging letter from the playwright, the script was returned, together with a photograph of "Sadie Masso:38–26–36:Just the Thing to Liven Up your Stag Night or Rugby Club Dinner", in an envelope without a stamp on it. At this point, that infallible source of advice, his wife's mother, told Malcolm Harris that she was sure she had seen something about a play-writing competition in some magazine she'd been reading at the hairdresser's, why didn't he go in for that? Painstaking research having tracked down the competition, sponsored by a local Arts Festival in the Midlands, the playwright had received his application form and copy of the rules. Obeying these implicitly, he had sent off his manuscript, together with the stamps for return postage and the entrance fee of one pound, and sat and waited. Four months later, he received back through the post a copy of *Psychosymbiosis*, a Monodrama by George Walsh. Repeated letters to the adjudicating committee of the Arts Festival, trying to retrieve the right manuscript, elicited no response.

Eighteen months had now passed since Malcolm Harris had completed *The Hooded Owl*, and so far there was no evidence that anyone vaguely connected with the professional theatre had even read it. The playwright was gloomily resigning himself to spending the rest of his days teaching history to recalcitrant adolescents, but the confidence of his wife, who had read the play, and his wife's mother, who hadn't, would not allow him to give up. His wife's mother had heard some successful playwright or maybe it was a producer talking on the radio she thought perhaps on *Woman's Hour* and saying that nowadays a successful play needed a star name, so often the star's interest came first. This suggestion coincided with Malcolm Harris reading a letter to *The Times* about VAT on theatre tickets from that popular British film and television star, Michael Banks. Since the letter gave his address, and since Michael Banks, in the playwright's wildest fantasies, would have been ideal casting for the main part, Malcolm Harris took his courage in both hands and sent *The Hooded Owl* off to the star. Needless to say, Michael Banks didn't read it, but, being an amiable old boy, he passed it on to his agent, whose organisation had a Plays Department. They didn't read it either, but a girl on the switchboard was having a brief affair with a young man who wanted to be a theatrical producer and claimed to be "on the look-out for a good property", so she passed it on to him. The young man read the play, recognised its potential, and bought an option to produce it within six months for a sum which delighted Malcolm Harris, but which would have appalled his agent, had he had one.

The young producer's name was Paul Lexington, and he then set about finding a theatre that would put the play on.

The Hooded Owl was an expensive production for the average provincial company. Though it only had a cast of eight and its contemporary setting limited the Wardrobe costs, it did require three solid representational sets, a very big outlay for a three-week run. Whereas a theatre might spread its budget to allow that kind of expenditure on a certain crowd-puller like a Shakespeare or the annual pantomime, it was very unlikely to invest so much in the uncertainties of a new play by an unknown playwright. Money was tight enough, and no provincial theatre wanted to hazard its local authority or Arts Council grants by rash speculation.

But this was where Paul Lexington had something to offer. He had money. No one quite knew where it came from; he always spoke airily of "my investors", but he gave no clue to their identity. And no one knew how much he could raise, though from the confidence of his tone, the amount seemed to be infinite.

So this was the deal that he offered round the provincial theatre companies during the spring and summer of 1979: if they would put on a production of *The Hooded Owl*, a good play for which he held an option, he would invest the necessary extra production costs for the expensive sets and, ideally, the import of a star name. Then, if the play did transfer to the West End, his production company would present it and the originating company would be credited and receive a small percentage. If it didn't transfer, then the theatre would have had a more expensive production than their normal budget could run to, and Paul Lexington and his investors would have lost their money.

Only Paul Lexington himself knew how many companies had been offered the deal and turned it down before he got to the Prince's Theatre, Taunton, but common sense dictated that he must have tried the better-known ones nearer London first. The chances of getting all the people necessary for a transfer, the London theatre managers and the big investors (whose aid, in spite of Paul Lexington's confident assurances, would almost definitely be needed), diminished the further one got away from the metropolis.

However, the producer was determined to get the show on and was

11

confident enough of the property to think it could make the transfer, even from this West Country base, whose record of getting shows into the West End was not remarkable. (In fact, it had never in its history had an original production transfer, though a few shows had passed weeks there during their pre-London tours.)

But there was a new Artistic Director at the Prince's Theatre, a young man called Peter Hickton, whose confidence at least matched that of Paul Lexington. He had got the Taunton job some six years out of Cambridge and was determined to maintain his whizz-kid image and make a mark on the theatre nationally. He was ambitious to make the Prince's Theatre a power-base and incubator of productions for London, in the way that the Royal Exchange, Manchester, and the Arts Theatre, Cambridge, had become in recent years. So, when Paul Lexington arrived with his proposal, Peter Hickton was already looking for a show with transfer potential.

His one condition for backing the production was predictable: that he should direct it. If that was agreed, he was prepared to put all his energies, even down to the *enfant terrible* tantrums that his track-record required of him, into persuading the Plays Selection Committee that *The Hooded Owl* should be one of the productions in the 1979–80 season at the Prince's Theatre, Taunton.

Paul Lexington at first demurred. He had hoped to get a director of greater stature for his production, but he soon had to face facts. Peter Hickton was the only Artistic Director who had shown enthusiasm for the project and, if Paul Lexington Productions were to get their first major show under way at all, there would have to be compromises. (And it was not lost on the producer that Peter Hickton's residence at Taunton meant directing the show would be part of his job. Sure, he'd have to be on some percentage when the play got to the West End, but at least a director's fee would be saved for the try-out)

So the two ambitious young men came to an agreement, and Peter Hickton set to work on the Plays Selection Committee. His success was not total. He managed to get a commitment that the Prince's Theatre should do *The Hooded Owl*, but he could not persuade them to do it in the 1979–80 season. He tried all his tricks, being sarcastic, going dead quiet, shouting, walking out of the meeting, even threatening (carefully) to resign: but the best date he could come up with was September, 1980. Seeing that to protest further would be pushing his luck, he agreed with bad grace that *The Hooded Owl* should be the first production of the 1980–81 season.

12

Paul Lexington didn't welcome this delay to his plans, but he was a realist and he wanted to get the show on, so he accepted it. He rang Malcolm Harris to say he had some good news and some bad news: the good news—that the play would definitely go into production at the Prince's Theatre, Taunton; the bad news—that it wouldn't happen for another year. He did not mention to the playwright that the six-month option he had bought on the play would be some eight months out of date at the proposed production date, nor did he offer more money to renew the option. He knew that Malcolm Harris was still in a flush of naive excitement about the play actually being produced and wasn't thinking about money.

So for a year Paul Lexington continued with his other activities, whatever they might be. Nobody knew. Maybe he mounted another Music Hall tour, maybe a pantomime. Maybe he involved his investors in some other production; maybe he made contacts with London theatre managements, so that the delay should be kept to a minimum when the production actually happened.

The one thing he was known to have done during that period was to try to get a star name for *The Hooded Owl*. As with theatre companies, only he knew how many he approached with the script, how many refusals he got, how many tentative agreements dependent on dates and money. There were two main male parts and one female, so presumably stars of both sexes were approached.

All that was known was the result of his machinations. A fortnight before rehearsals were due to start, which was the time when Charles Paris was engaged to play the second male lead, it was bruited about in the business that the female lead was to be played by a young lady who had recently, "in order to concentrate on her career as a serious actress", left the cast of the interminably-long-running television soap opera, *Cruises*.

The fact that she wasn't much of an actress, serious or any other sort, was irrelevant. The audience would flock to see her. It didn't matter if she just stood on stage, they would still love her. (In fact, people who had worked with her thought it might be better if she *did* just stand on stage; they knew the hazards of trying to push her beyond her range.)

Once Paul Lexington had his star name, he was happy to fall in with Peter Hickton's suggestions for the rest of the cast. So long as they were cheap, competent and available in the event of a transfer, he didn't much mind who they were. As a result, Peter Hickton cast largely from

13

his regular Taunton company; he knew them, they worshipped him, and he fancied himself in the role of star-maker.

In the lead he cast Alex Household, an actor in his late forties, who had had early success, then a rather bad patch culminating in a complete breakdown, but was now coming back, in the view of Peter Hickton, twenty years his junior, "stronger than ever".

In the part of the daughter, Peter Hickton cast Lesley-Jane Decker, an actress eight years his junior, who he thought had "enormous potential". And the way he looked at her didn't suggest he thought that potential was limited to the stage.

For the part of Alex's failed brother, Peter reckoned he had had a brainwave. There was no one in the regular Taunton company of the right age, but he remembered an actor he had worked with when Assistant Director at Colchester, who had exactly the right "smell of failure" that the part required. Peter rang the guy's agent and found, to his delight, that he was free.

To the agent in question, Maurice Skellern, his client's "freeness" was no surprise. Charles Paris's engagement diary was a joke on the level of all those corny old lines about *The Kosher Book of Pork Recipes*, *Britain's Economic Miracle* or *The Pope's Book of Birth Control*. "I've sorted out a great job for you, Charles," the agent asserted when he rang.

"Oh yes?" Charles had replied sceptically.

"Sure. Great new play called *The Head Owl*."

"Where?"

"Taunton."

"Ah."

"Director asked for you specially."

"Oh."

"Said he wanted someone who really smelt of failure."

"Thank you, Maurice."

So it was that Charles Paris joined the cast of *The Hooded Owl*.

It was the day before rehearsals started that the agent of the former *Cruises* star rang to say that she had just signed up to do a series for West End Television of a new sit. com. set in a lingerie shop and called *Knickers*; so, because that was going to keep her very busy, she had flown off the day before to Kenya for a safari holiday. And no, sorry, she hadn't actually signed *The Hooded Owl* contract.

Frantic phoning ensued. Paul Lexington tried in vain to produce a star in twenty-four hours, but eventually had to accept Peter Hickton's casting of Salome Search, a Taunton regular, "who's awfully solid, Paul, and, you know, has never really had the breaks, but could be massive."

So it was that, while the former *Cruises* star pointed her camera at world-weary rhino, her predestined dressing room at the Prince's Theatre, Taunton, was shared on the first night of *The Hooded Owl* by Alex Household and Charles Paris.

CHAPTER TWO

NERVES, LIKE hopes, Charles found, didn't go away, however long he worked in the theatre. The fact that he had survived a few hundred first nights did not make each new one any easier. In some ways it made it more difficult; he now had more experience of the things that could go wrong than he had in his twenties, and so the dark side of his imagination had more to work on.

But two things delayed the full impact of his nerves about the opening of *The Hooded Owl*. The first was having a large part, a fortune that was not often his lot. He began to realise how stars could remain cool right up till the first night. Their responsibility was greater, but the mechanics of learning all their lines and rehearsing kept them pretty busy. It was those with small parts and long gaps in rehearsal who had time to sit around twitching over endless diuretic cups of coffee.

The other factor which staved off the assault of nerves was the work-rate Peter Hickton demanded of his cast. Because most of them had worked with him so much, they knew what to expect, that he would rehearse every waking hour (and a good few normally allocated to sleep). Equity rules about maximum hours were ignored. There was an Equity representative in the cast, duly elected by the rest, but he was one of the Peter Hickton rep. too, so he made no demur.

Peter Hickton was one of those people who gained ascendancy over others by demonstrating how little sleep he needed. Charles, whose ideal was a whisky-sodden eight hours, found this was a contest in which he did not wish to participate, but he had no alternative. He couldn't turn up for a nine o'clock call in the morning and complain that he hadn't finished rehearsing till one the night before, when he knew that the director had been up till four working on the lighting plan.

Charles also found this relentless rehearsal made serious inroads into his drinking time, a part of the day he had always regarded as sacrosanct. He wasn't an alcoholic (he kept telling himself), but he did enjoy a drink, and he found resorting to a half-bottle of Bell's in his pocket somewhat undignified. Apart from anything else, it gave his antiquated sports jacket a lop-sided look. And it tended to clink against things. Also it gave the wrong impression. When Salome Search caught him one day taking a surreptitious swig in the Green Room, she gave him a look that showed she had got a completely false idea of his relationship with drink. She obviously regarded it as a till-death-do-us-part marriage, whereas he liked to think of it more as a casual affair, in which either partner could drift off at will (though, when he came to think of it, neither often did).

Peter Hickton's rehearsal schedule (probably a misnomer for a process that was simply continuous) intensified towards the end. The Monday night's Tech. Run, which followed a full day in the rehearsal room, finished at three-thirty a.m. As a special concession, the next morning's call for notes was not until nine-thirty, then rehearsal of odd scenes continued till it was time for the evening's Dress Rehearsal, which, though intended to be played as per performance, did not end till a quarter to two a.m. Because of this, Peter Hickton demanded a second Dress Rehearsal, on the Wednesday afternoon before the first night. This was followed by notes, taking everyone right up to "the half" (the time half an hour before curtain-up, by which all members of the cast have to be in the theatre).

So Charles didn't even have time for the half-hour in the pub over a couple of large Bell's, which he regarded as such an essential preparation for the full realisation of his art.

What was more, he was down to about half an inch in his pocket-bottle thanks to the pressures of the previous days. He had been sure there'd at least be time for him to nip out and buy a replacement.

But there wasn't. And all the A.S.M.s and hangers-on were too busy to have this important commission delegated to them.

It was a serious situation.

And it didn't improve the half-hour before curtain-up, when all the pent-up nerves came crashing in with devastating force. Normally he could control the incipient nausea and limit the number of rushes to the lavatory by judiciously-spaced doses of Bell's whisky, but now he felt as if he was having a leg off without anaesthetic.

He drained the half-bottle to attain some sort of stability, but five minutes later, when something started doing macramé with his intestines, he wished he had saved it.

17

Alex Household's method of building up to a performance did not involve alcohol. He did not believe in the use of stimulants, being an advocate of the use of the mind's internal resources to control the waywardness of the body. It was part of an elaborate philosophy he had developed from reading the first chapters of a few paperbacks about Eastern Religion and talking to other actors over cups of jasmine tea.

His build-up method involved lying dead straight over three chairs, with the head free and lolling back, and breathing deeply. A deep intake of air sounding like a gas central heating boiler igniting, a long pause, and then exhalation over a muttered phrase, which may have been some potent *mantra*, but to the casual observer sounded like "Rub-a-dub-a-dub-a-dub-a-dub."

Charles was becoming a decreasingly casual observer as the half-hour ticked away and his nerves were twisted tighter. Alex's charade didn't help. Charles, normally most accommodating about the foibles of others, began to think sharing the dressing room might have its drawbacks.

Alex was that very common theatrical type, a faddish actor. He believed in vegetarianism, transcendental meditation, homeopathy, transmigration, the occult and a variety of other semi-digested notions. Alex was always talking about communion with nature and being at one with the world. He had a habit of producing herbal snacks in the dressing room, seeds, grasses, nettles and other less identifiable greenery. He had read a few chapters of a book called *Food for Free*, and kept going on about "the earth's plenty".

Normally, Charles could accept all this with good humour—after all, he did quite like the man—but, as he again suffered the interminable pause between the intake and the inevitable "Rub-a-dub-a-dub-a-dub-a-dub" he thought he was going to scream or lash out. To avert both these dangers, he left the dressing room to go to the lavatory, though he couldn't resist slamming the door as he went.

In the corridor he met Lesley-Jane Decker, whose arms were full of purple tissue-wrapped parcels. She was an attractive red-head of about twenty, still full of breathless excitement about actually "being in the theatre". She was quite talented, and devoutly believed Paul Lexington's and Peter Hickton's conviction that *The Hooded Owl* was going to sweep triumphantly into the West End and make them all stars.

It had been obvious from rehearsal that Peter Hickton fancied her, but whether he had got anywhere, Charles could not judge. In fact, he couldn't imagine how the director's rehearsal schedule would leave any time for thoughts of sex, though, of course, all things were possible.

On balance, Charles thought that probably nothing had developed. Apart from the logistics, Lesley-Jane was so naive and bubbly, he could not imagine her keeping quiet about a love affair. He even suspected that she might be that remarkable rarity, a theatrical virgin.

And it was more likely that Peter Hickton was saving his assault on her for the less hectic time when the play was actually running. There would be two and a half weeks then, which should give the young director plenty of time.

"Oh, Charles darling, this is for you." Lesley-Jane thrust one of the packages into his hands.

"Oh," he said blankly.

"First-night present."

"Ah." Theatrical camp, he thought. What would it be? A fluffy toy? No, felt too hard. A plaster statuette of a pierrot? Yes, that'd be the sort of thing. "Oh, er, thank you. How are you feeling?"

She opened her green eyes wide. "Scared witless, darling. Paul says he's hoping there'll be some people from London out front."

"Oh really?" Charles had heard that a few too many times to get very excited about it.

"And, even worse . . ." She paused dramatically.

"What?"

"My mother's come down from London to see it."

"Is that bad? Is she awful?"

"No, she's an absolute angel. But she's got awfully high standards. Used to be in the business, you know."

"Oh." The need to get to the lavatory was suddenly strong again. "If you'll excuse me . . ."

"Yes. Is Alex in the dressing room?"

"Sure."

Sitting on the lavatory, Charles opened his first-night present. Oh, good, that girl would go far. He took back all his thoughts about her naiveté and theatrical camp.

It was a quarter bottle of champagne. He drained it gratefully.

As he went back to his dressing room, he met the author of *The Hooded Owl*, hanging around in the corridor like a schoolboy outside the headmaster's study. The expression of agony on Malcolm Harris's pallid face made Charles's own nerves seem less crippling.

"Don't worry. It'll be all right. It's a good play."

19

"Do you really think so?" The schoolmaster's pouncing on this crumb of praise was almost pathetic.

"Yes, of course it is. We wouldn't have put in all this work on it if it hadn't been."

"Oh, I do hope so. It's just no one seems to have talked about anything for the past few days except the bits that don't work and all the technical problems it raises and . . ."

Poor sap. Yes, it must have been strange for him, religiously attending the last week of rehearsals, and knowing nothing about the workings of the theatre. Everyone would be far too busy to waste time assuring the author that his play worked; there would be a lot of complaint about its inadequacies and difficulties. Anyone who had had a play produced before would have been prepared for that; but for Malcolm Harris, snatched from teaching the Causes of the Thirty Years' War to fourteen-year-olds, it must all have been a profound culture shock. Charles felt guilty for not having realised earlier what the author had been suffering.

"It'll work. Really."

Malcolm made a grimace that might have been intended for a smile. "Maybe. My main worry is everyone getting the lines right."

That's what every author wants, thought Charles. And occasionally they get it, though most actors are highly skilled in the art of paraphrase.

"I do hope Alex gets that big speech about the Hooded Owl itself right. I mean, that is the key to the play, and he got the rhythms all wrong this afternoon."

"Don't worry," Charles soothed. Poor old Alex was having a bit of difficulty with the lines, he thought complacently.

"Oh, and Charles, could you watch your line at the end of Act One."

"What?"

"At the Dress Rehearsal, you said, 'I'll tell you one thing—it's the last time I'll come running.'"

"So? Isn't that right?"

"No. It should be, 'I'll tell you *something* . . .'."

Oh really! thought Charles. Bloody authors!

But he didn't say it. Instead he asked, "Anyone out front tonight?"

"Oh, just my wife and my wife's mother."

"Ah." Then, reassuringly, "And maybe lots of impresarios and film producers waiting to snap up the rights. How would you feel about a film offer on the play?"

20

"Oh, I'd . . . I'd get my agent to deal with it," replied the author, with an unsuccessful attempt at insouciance.

Still, good. At least he'd got an agent. Slowly he was sorting himself out.

Charles looked at his watch. Twenty past seven. "Must just go in and check the old slap," he said, gesturing to his make-up.

"Yes, I'll come in and wish Alex all the best."

Charles opened the dressing room door to discover that Alex Household had stopped his "Rub-a-dub-a-dub-a-dub-a-dub" routine. In fact, though they sprang apart quickly, he appeared to be doing his giving-Lesley-Jane-Decker-a-cuddle-on-his-knee routine. Well, there's a novelty, thought Charles.

Alex tapped Lesley-Jane on the bottom in a way that was meant to suggest the contact had just been theatrical excess, but he didn't convince Charles.

"And thank you so much for the ginseng, darling," said Alex, to reinforce the impression of casual contact.

Ginseng. Of course. It would be. Lesley-Jane had got Alex's number all right.

"Um . . ." Malcolm Harris began awkwardly. "Um, Alex, just came in to say good luck—"

"Oh Lord!" shouted the actor. "For Christ's sake!"

The author looked mystified by the outburst.

"Don't you know anything, you bloody amateur?"

"I don't understand . . ."

"You mustn't say what you've just said."

"What? I musn't say good—"

"Don't say it again!" Alex shrieked. "It's bad luck."

"Well, what should I say?"

"Oh Lord—break a leg or . . . anything but that!"

Charles should have remembered: amongst Alex Household's other fads was devout observance of all the theatrical superstitions.

Malcolm Harris's minimal confidence had now deserted him completely.

"I'm sorry. I don't know these—"

"No, you don't know anything!" snapped Alex. "Don't even know how to write a decent play!"

In a second the author's hand clenched into a fist and was raised to strike. But in the fractional pause that preceded the blow, the Stage Manager's calming voice came over the loudspeaker.

"Beginners, Act One, please."

Malcolm Harris lowered his fist, glowered at the lead actor of his precious play, and scurried off to find the pass-door to join his wife and his wife's mother in the auditorium.

Alex Household, Lesley-Jane Decker and Charles Paris hugged each other wordlessly, and passed through the corridor to the stage.

The eruption of applause as the final curtain fell left no one in any doubt that *The Hooded Owl* had worked, at least for the good burghers of Taunton. Whether it would work for the supposedly more sophisticated audience of the West End remained to be seen.

But for the cast there was no doubt about anything. Each of them had felt the momentum of the play build up through the evening, each of them had felt their doubts about its worth evaporate, each of them felt the relief of consummation after their exhausting preparations. They were all euphoric.

Charles and Alex tumbled back into the Number One dressing room, arms around each other's necks, giggling like schoolgirls. "Yippee, yippee. It works, it works!" cried Alex.

They both felt emotionally drained—the parts they played were taxing—but lifted above exhaustion on to a high like drunkenness.

As Charles became aware of this, he realised that he had given a performance—and a good one—on an alcoholic intake of only a swig of Bell's and a quarter bottle of champagne. This was something of a record for him, and momentarily the heretical thought traversed his mind that maybe his talent could flourish without constant irrigation.

Mind you, he really needed a drink now.

As if in answer to his thought, Paul Lexington poked his head round the dressing room door. "Terrific, both of you! We have a hit on our hands, babies! Soon as you're out of your cossies, up to the bar. Drinks are on me tonight!"

"That's very generous of you, Paul," said Charles.

"Oh, it's nothing. I'd laid it on for anyone who came down from London."

"And has anyone come?"

A shadow passed over the producer's boyish face. "No, not tonight. I expect they'll be along later in the week."

But he was incapable of pessimism. "Don't worry, I'll be on the phone first thing in the morning. Tell 'em the quality of what they're missing. They'll be falling over themselves trying to snap this one up."

At that moment Lesley-Jane Decker burst in, as effervescent as the champagne she had handed out. She threw her arms round Alex Household's neck. "God, you were wonderful tonight."

"Oh Lord, praise, praise," he said, with a shrug.

"You were super too." Paul Lexington patted Lesley-Jane on the shoulder. "See you up in the bar."

"Terrific."

As the producer turned to leave, he was met in the doorway by a tall lady in a light-brown fur coat. She looked as if she was in her forties, but slightly over-elaborate make-up and hair that had been helped to recapture its former redness, made putting an exact date on her difficult.

"Excuse me," she apologised in a rich, elocuted voice. "I don't want to intrude."

She was looking at Alex and Lesley-Jane still clasped together, a sight for which she seemed to have slight distaste.

The young actress turned at the voice and rushed across to the older woman. "Mummy! Mummy, *do* come and meet everyone."

Paul Lexington, after being introduced, nodded politely and said he hoped she'd join them for a drink in the bar. Alex Household said he was enchanted, *but* enchanted to see her at last, he'd heard so much about her.

"And, Mummy, this is—"

"Ah, but I know you, don't I, Charles?"

Charles Paris looked up warily at the woman's face. Maybe there was something vaguely familiar about it, but he couldn't for the life of him say where he had seen her before. "Um . . ."

"Long time ago, darling . . ."

"Oh . . . er . . ." He was going to need a bit more of a clue than that.

Malcolm Harris blundered in through the door flanked by ferret-faced women who had to be his wife and his wife's mother, and there was a pause for more introductions.

"Wonderful play, Malcolm," Alex cooed. "Oh Lord, what a wonderful play."

But the diversion didn't let Charles off the hook. "Have you placed me yet?" asked Lesley-Jane's mother seductively.

"Um, no . . ." he had to admit, wondering whether their previous encounter had been under embarrassing circumstances.

"You remember Cheltenham . . . ?" she nudged.

"What? Cheltenham Rep? Back in the early sixties?"

"Sssh." She raised an elegantly manicured finger to her lips. "Don't let's talk dates. But yes, Cheltenham Rep. it was."

Given a context, he did begin to place her. "Oh yes." But he still couldn't for the life of him remember what her name was.

She seemed to realise this, and gave in. "Valerie Cass."

"Of course! Valerie Cass! Well, how are you? Talk about long time, no see."

As he brought out the platitudes of recognition, he placed her exactly. Yes, of course, early sixties, Cheltenham, young actress, playing *ingénue* roles. Now he knew the connection, he remembered that she had had that same quality of naive enthusiasm that Lesley-Jane demonstrated. Not as good an actress, though. No, his recollection was that Valerie Cass had been a pretty bad actress.

As if to apologise for this thought, he continued fulsomely, "Valerie Cass! You know, you haven't changed a bit. Have you got a picture up in the attic that grows old instead of you?"

This was the right approach—or at least the approach she liked. She fluttered coquettishly.

"I've followed your career with interest, Charles. Read *Stage* every week, you know."

Oh, thought Charles, there must have been a few thousand weeks when you've searched it in vain for any mention of me. "Are you still in the business?"

"Oh goodness me, no, Charles. I gave up when I married Lesley's father. Had my time fully occupied bringing up my baby girl."

"Yes, I'm sure." It seemed a good solution to Charles. Valerie Cass had probably been quite good as a mother; whereas, had she stayed in the theatre, it would only have been a matter of time before her lack of talent had been exposed.

"No, no, Lesley-Jane carries on the theatrical tradition in our family. Of course, I give her any help I can, but . . ." She shrugged. "I'm afraid my career was cut short. So I'm just left with my dreams of what might have been."

Charles hoped, for her sake, the dreams weren't accurate. No, no doubt like his own, they were pure wish-fulfilment.

He still felt apologetic for not having recognised her. "Sorry, it was so out of context. I mean, Lesley-Jane's name gave me no clue."

"No, she got that from her father," said Valerie Cass rather tartly.

Mother and daughter, and Malcolm Harris and his womenfolk eventually left the two actors to change out of their costumes.

24

"Last one in the bar's a sissy," said Charles, the euphoric giggliness returning.

They both plunged for the door and, as they collided, Charles felt something heavy in Alex's jacket pocket thump against him.

"You great fraud! All your talk of 'no stimulants' and you're another of the flask-in-pocket brigade!'

"Oh no," said Alex Household gravely. "It's not a flask."

"Then what . . . ?"

"I got mugged last year, walking back from the theatre in Birmingham." His voice became unsteady. "I got beaten up. It won't happen again. I never go out after dark without this."

He withdrew his hand from his pocket. It was clasped around the butt of a Smith and Wesson Chiefs Special revolver.

CHAPTER THREE

THE LOCAL paper thought *The Hooded Owl* was a success. It even raved about it. The last sentence of the notice read, "It is rarely that down here in Taunton we are treated to a show of such excellence. I urge everyone to go and see *The Hooded Owl* now, before you have to pay fares to London and West End prices for the privilege."

So, as far as the local paper was concerned, the transfer was a certainty. Unfortunately, it wasn't local papers that arranged such things. It was London theatre managements and, at the end of the first week's run, even Paul Lexington's unpuncturable buoyancy could not hide the fact that no one relevant had been down to see the show. Still, as he kept asserting cheerfully, two weeks to go, and a lot could happen in two weeks.

The local paper review, as well as backing the whole show, was also extremely gratifying to Alex Household and Charles Paris. The sentence which kept recurring in both their minds for some days, was this: "After witnessing acting of such power and emotional truth, it is hard to imagine why these two actors are not considerably better known than they are."

Exactly, they both thought, that's what we've been saying for years.

For Charles, the review was particularly welcome. For one thing, the sort of part he usually played didn't often get reviewed. And for another, on the past three occasions when critics had deigned to mention him, their comments had been as follows:

"Charles Paris was an odd choice for the part of the solicitor"— *Guardian*

"Charles Paris wandered through the play like one of Bo-Peep's sheep looking for its tail"—*Evening Standard*

And—"Among the rest of the cast was Charles Paris"—*The Stage*

In spite of the fact that nothing was happening on the transfer front, the cast could not keep down their optimism. The experience of playing in a

26

success, endorsed nightly by the audience's reaction, was an invigorating one, and Paul Lexington's so-far-groundless confidence was infectious.

"You know," said Alex Household, as he made up on the Tuesday evening of the second week, "I think it is going to work. I think we will make it."

Charles grinned. Closer acquaintance with the other actor had increased his liking for the man. His antagonistic feelings of the first night had just been the product of nerves. Now he found that, so long as he arranged to be out of the dressing room for the "Rub-a-dub-a-dub-a-dub-a-dub" routine, he could cohabit with Alex quite happily. He had also found, to his surprise, that Alex had some sense of humour about his various fads and would even respond to gentle teasing on the subject.

"Yes, it's going to happen," Alex continued. "I feel my luck is due for a change."

"Hmm. I gather you've had a fairly rough few years."

"You can say that again. First I had a long patch out of work, then my marriage broke up—are you married, Charles?"

Difficult question, really. He had married Frances back in 1951, and they weren't divorced. They had a grown-up daughter, Juliet. On the other hand, he had walked out after ten years and, though he still saw Frances and felt a lot of ill-defined emotion for her, theirs was not what most people meant by a marriage.

"Um, not unmarried," he replied cagily.

Not that Alex was really interested. He continued his own catalogue of disasters. "Then I had the breakdown. It was an awful time. I went through everything—drugs, psychotherapy, the lot.

"But that was three years ago. Everything's going to be all right now. I am going on on that assumption. I've just bought this new flat in town, so a nice West End run is just what the mortgage and I need."

"And if the transfer doesn't happen . . . ?"

"Treason, Charles. Don't even say it."

"No, I mean have you got another job lined up after this one?"

Alex shook his head. "You?"

"Good Lord, no."

A tap on the door prefaced the bursting-in of Lesley-Jane Decker, even more effervescent than usual. She threw her arms round Alex's neck and looked at him in his mirror. "Have you heard, darling?"

"What?"

"Wonderful news."

27

"Your mother's gone back to London?"

Lesley-Jane giggled, then, guiltily, stopped. "No, no, Alex. Denis Thornton's in tonight."

"Really?" said both the actors together.

The name meant a great deal. Denis Thornton had been a successful juvenile in a long string of undemanding West End comedies, but had of latter years turned his talents and money towards management. Though he would still occasionally come back for a sixth-month run in a tailor-made comedy vehicle, most of his energies now went into Lanthorn Productions, which he owned with his partner, Gerard Langley. They were lessees of three or four London theatres and, in difficult times, made commercial theatre work. The shows they put on may have contributed little to the nation's cultural heritage, but they certainly brought in the coach parties.

"Ah." Alex looked complacent. "I heard that show at the King's was doing fairly bad business."

"King's would be a bit big for this, wouldn't it?" said Charles. "It's more for your grand musicals and . . ."

"It'd do . . ." Alex preened himself with a hint of self-parody. "Yes, I wouldn't mind having my name in lights above the title at the King's."

"I'm sure you will, darling." Lesley-Jane kissed the top of his head. "Got to go. I left Mummy in my dressing room. See you."

"See you."

She fizzed out. Charles gestured towards the door with his head.

"She part of your new start, Alex?"

"Why not? As I say, about time my luck changed."

"Hmm. I thought Peter Hickton had earmarked her."

"So did he, dear, but experience does tell, you know. It's my belief that all young girls should have their first affair with an older man. Anyway, dear Peter's always so busy . . ."

"You've been pretty busy too. Don't know how you've had time or opportunity to . . ."

"Time, my dear Charles, can always be made. And you forget that Lesley-Jane and I joined the company at the end of last season. As for opportunity . . . well, always sort out a bolt-hole for yourself, Charles."

"What do you mean?"

But he only got an enigmatic and rather smug smile by way of answer.

"Lesley-Jane's a sweet kid," Charles volunteered magnanimously.

"Oh yes. Only one thing wrong with her."

"What's that?"

"She's not an orphan."

"Ah, doesn't the lovely Valerie approve of you?"

"Not really."

"Because you're too old?"

"No, I think simply because I'm a man."

Charles nodded and started to powder down his make-up.

"Still, sod the lot of them!" said Alex Household with sudden venom. "I am going to win through. I am going to have all the successful things I should have had years ago. And none of the buggers are going to stop me!"

Once again Charles detected the unstable note of paranoia in the other's voice.

There was a call for all cast on stage at the "half" for the next day's matinée. Most of them reckoned they had a pretty shrewd idea of what it was for.

And sure enough, when Paul Lexington addressed them, his first two words were the ones which had been the cause of much discussion and speculation since the previous evening.

"Denis Thornton," he announced, "as you may or may not know, came down to see the show last night. And I have some good news for you—he liked it!"

The cast burst into shouts of delight, but cut them off sharply, waiting to hear what followed from this.

"And basically what has happened is—he has offered us a theatre to transfer the show to the West End!"

This was greeted with more euphoria. As it died away, Salome Search, who plumed herself on knowing a bit about the mechanics of "going in" to the West End, having once spent a week in the chorus of an ill-fated musical at the Apollo, asked, "Does that mean Lanthorn Productions will be presenting the show?"

"Oh no. I will be presenting the show. Denis's company will just be renting us the theatre. It gives us a lot more freedom than if Lanthorn actually took over."

And a lot more chance to fail, thought Charles cynically.

"So when will we be going in to the King's?" asked Alex.

"Ah, it's not the King's," said Paul. "No, Denis reckons the King's is far too big for this show. We'd get lost in there. No, he's offering us the Variety."

"Oh," said all the cast at the same moment, trying not to sound disappointed.

The Variety Theatre had had a chequered history. It was called a West End theatre, but its position, in Macklin Street, was a little too far from Shaftesbury Avenue for the designation to sound convincing. It had been a popular Music Hall venue before the First World War, and come back to prominence in the fifties with a series of intimate revues. Since then it had justified its name by the variety of managements who had tried to make a go of it and the variety of fare they had presented there. Mime shows, light shows, nude shows, drag shows had all been washed up there as theatrical fashions ebbed and flowed. Religious rock musicals had followed on modern dance extravaganzas; one-man shows based on eighteenth century letters had succeeded abortive attempts to revive the art of stage revue; poetry readings had drawn the same size audiences as South African jail diaries; laser shows, a punk rock musical and a gay version of *Romeo and Juliet* in black leather had all been tried, and failed.

It was currently occupied by an entertainment based on Maori song and dance, which had somehow maintained its sickly life there for nearly three months.

"Now I know what you're all thinking," said Paul Lexington hastily. "That the Variety hasn't had a success for the past twenty years. Don't worry. *The Hooded Owl* is going to change all that. Listen, Denis Thornton has just taken over the lease and he's no fool. He's been looking for a property to reopen the theatre under his management and we are it. If we go to the Variety, we'll go in with maximum publicity and really put the place back on the map!"

The cast were so willing to believe the best that Paul Lexington's rabble-rousing techniques worked and they instantly forgot their reservations and shouted again with excitement. Yes, of course they could succeed where others had failed. They were good. *The Hooded Owl* was good. Not only were they going to take the West End by storm, they were going to redefine its boundaries.

Alex Household adjusted his question. "So when do we go in to the Variety?"

"If all goes well, we'd open there in about four weeks. 30th October."

The date seemed very near and was greeted with renewed cheering.

"Now there are a few things to sort out," the producer continued. "I'll

30

have to go back to my investors. Because of the guarantees required I'm going to have to raise a bit more money. But that shouldn't be any problem."

In the ecstatic mood of the company, no one was so cynical as to think of the last sentence as understatement. In order to be allowed to go into the West End, Paul would have to put up in advance all of the rehearsal money and two weeks' running costs for the production. The rehearsal money would be paid back when the show opened, the rest when it closed. Couldn't be that much, the cast all thought; as Paul said, it shouldn't be any problem.

"So I'm going to be very busy for the next couple of weeks, rushing around, raising the loot. I'm also going to be getting lots more people down to see the show, so remember—give of your best every night, you never know who's going to be in.

"But basically—don't worry. I'll sort it all out. And *The Hooded Owl* is going in to the West End!"

Malcolm Harris reappeared for the Friday performance of the second week. No one had really noticed his absence, just as no one had really noticed his presence when he had been there. Presumably the previous weekend his ferret-faced women had taken him back to his ferret-faced children, and he had spent the week teaching history.

He came in to the Number One dressing room after the performance. Alex Household looked at him in the mirror and asked, "Well, happy with the way your little masterpiece is shaping up?"

"Not very," the author replied awkwardly.

"Why not?"

"Well, the lines are all over the place."

"What do you mean?"

"Well, I'm sorry, Alex, but I have to say it— you're really killing the big speech about the Hooded Owl."

"Killing it? Oh, come on. That's the high spot of the evening. Not a sweet-paper rustles, even the chronic bronchitics are cured at that moment."

"Well, of course. That's how it's meant to be. But you're not saying the lines as written. Again tonight you said, 'And this bird has seen it all, lived through it all, silently, impassively.'"

"That's what I say every night."

"Well, you shouldn't. The line, as written, is, 'And this bird has lived through it all, has seen it all, impassively, in silence.'"

31

"Oh Lord—really! What difference does it make? I think my version flows better, actually, sounds more poetic."

"It's not meant to sound bloody poetic, for God's sake! It would be out of character for the father to sound poetic."

"Oh, look—"

Charles decided a tactical intervention might be in order. As if he had suddenly walked into the room and heard none of the preceding exchange, he asked naively, "What do you think of the news about the Variety, eh, Malcolm?"

"Oh, it's very encouraging," said the schoolmaster. "Salome told me before the show tonight."

Oh dear, that was a slip-up on Paul Lexington's part. The author should have been told as soon as the producer knew, not hear the rumour from a third party. Fortunately, though, Malcolm did not seem aggrieved. His ignorance of the theatre encompassed a great deal of humility (about everything except the actors getting his lines right).

"Do you think you can cope with fame and all those royalties?" asked Charles playfully.

The schoolmaster gave a shy smile. "I think I'll manage."

"Hmm. Make sure your agent sorts out a good deal for you. Remember this axiom of theatrical business—all managements are sharks."

"Oh, I'm sure it'll be all right."

"Who is your agent, by the way?"

Malcolm's smile grew broader. "That's the wonderful thing. When Paul heard I hadn't got an agent, he was shocked . . ."

"I should think so. And he recommended someone to you?"

"No, better than that, Charles. He said he'd represent me himself. Keep it all in the family, he said. Isn't that terrific?"

"And you've signed up with him?"

"You bet. And no messing about with short contracts. He's really showing his confidence in me and agreed to let me sign up for three years."

"Ah." It was all Charles could say. The damage was done; the contract was signed. He found it incredible that every day produced new innocents to fall for the oldest tricks in the business. But there was no point now in telling Malcolm the folly of signing up with the same person as agent and manager, no point in making him think what would happen when he was in dispute with the management and needed an agent to represent his interests. The schoolmaster would have to find out the hard way.

But the knowledge did put Paul Lexington's image in a different light. If he was capable of that sort of old-fashioned sharp practice, maybe his other dealings should be watched with a wary eye.

Further speculation about the producer was interrupted by the ebullient entrance of Lesley-Jane Decker. "Alex, Alex, have you heard? Bobby Anscombe was in tonight."

"Was he?" said Alex and Charles in impressed unison.

"Who?" asked Malcolm Harris ignorantly.

But his question didn't get an answer, so he sidled out into the corridor and away.

The answer he didn't get was that Bobby Anscombe was a very big theatrical backer, or "angel", whose instincts had directed his money into a string of lucrative hits. He was rich, shrewd, and prepared to take risks, to rush in, indeed, where other angels feared to tread. His style had paid off handsomely in the past, and the fact that he had come all the way to Taunton to see *The Hooded Owl* was the most encouraging boost so far for the transfer prospects.

Alex Household rubbed his hands slowly together. "That is very good news, Lesley-Jane, very good news."

"Yes, darling. Let's hope he liked it."

"I don't honestly see how he could have failed to." Alex's confidence these days seemed to be unassailable. He reached out and took Lesley-Jane's hand. "Tell me, do you fancy a *drive in the country* tomorrow morning? I could do with some fresh air."

The way he italicised the words showed they had some private meaning for the couple.

"Oh, I'd love to, darling, but I can't. Got to go to the station and meet Mummy."

"Oh Lord, is she coming down again?"

"She's terribly lonely in town with only Daddy for company."

"Of course." Alex turned back to his mirror and started rubbing grease on to his face.

"See you up in the bar?" asked Lesley-Jane tentatively.

"Possibly," said Alex Household.

"Oh yes," said Charles Paris.

He had a good few drinks inside him as he left the theatre. The quickest way back to his digs was by a path near the car park and, as he walked

33

along, he heard Paul Lexington's voice from the other side of a wall. "Good," it said. "Excellent. I'm delighted at your reaction."

"We'll talk on Monday about the points I made," said an unfamiliar voice, "but I think we can assume that, in principle, we have a deal."

"Terrific," said Paul Lexington's voice.

A car door slammed, a powerful engine started, and there was a screech of tyres. As Charles came to the end of the wall by the car park exit, he was nearly run over by a silver-grey Rolls Corniche.

As he watched it go off up the road, its BA registration left him in no doubt that it belonged to Bobby Anscombe.

And the conversation he had overheard left him in no doubt that Bobby Anscombe was going to back *The Hooded Owl*.

He didn't mention what he had overheard to anyone when he went in the next day for the Saturday matinée. After all, they'd all know soon enough when Paul made an official announcement.

But the Saturday passed and no official announcement was made.

The final week of the run began. The Monday passed, the Tuesday, the Wednesday, and still there was no official announcement. No one would say that the transfer was definite.

Paul Lexington was around that week, though he kept on rushing up to town for unspecified meetings. As the days went past his cheerful face began to look more strained and the shadows around his eyes deepened. His manner was still confident, and, if directly asked, he would say everything was going well, but the old conviction seemed to have gone.

The cast felt it too. As the time trickled away, there was less talk of the transfer, less fantasies of what they were going to do when they got to the West End, more discussion of other potential jobs. Though no one dared to put it into words, they were all losing their faith.

And by the Saturday night, when the run ended, the atmosphere was one of gloom. The final performance was good and was received with more adulation than ever by the Taunton audience, but all the cast could feel their dreams slipping away. It was over, the play was finished, the right people hadn't made the effort to come all the way from London to see it, *The Hooded Owl* was destined to begin and end its life at the Prince's Theatre, Taunton.

So the mood of the cast party, held in the bar after the last performance, was more appropriate to a wake than a celebration. Still no one would voice the awful truth that faced them, but everyone knew. Any gaiety there was was forced.

Alex Household looked stunned and uncomprehending. Charles Paris was glad to pull out his old armour of cynicism and don it once again. Serve him right. He was too old to be seduced by that sort of childish hope in the theatre. Never mind, his old stand-bys would see him through. Cynicism and alcohol. He made the decision to get paralytically drunk.

He found himself, not wholly of his own volition, talking to Valerie Cass, who had appeared for yet another weekend. "You see," she was saying, "one does lose so much by being married. I mean, realising one's full potential as a woman."

She was obviously making some sort of sexual manoeuvre, though he wasn't quite sure what. He tried to reconstruct their previous meeting back at Cheltenham. Had he made any sort of pass at her then? Was she trying to pick up some previous affair?

But no, surely not. Round that time he had been breaking off with Frances and it had, surprisingly, been a time of celibacy. No, if her motive was sexual, this was something new.

"Of course," she went on, "one wouldn't have had it any other way. I mean, bringing up a child can be very fulfilling, but occasionally, when one stops and thinks, one does realise the opportunities one has missed—I mean, both in career terms and . . . emotionally. I think there comes a point where one is justified in being a little selfish, in thinking of oneself and one's own priorities for a moment. Don't you?"

"Oh, er, yes," replied Charles uneasily.

She seemed almost to be offering herself to him, and Charles was not in the habit of turning up such offers. And she remained an attractive woman. But something in the desperation of her manner turned him off.

"I always thought you were the sort of man who understood a woman's needs," she murmured to him.

Definitely time to change the subject. He looked around the bar. "No sign of Paul, is there?"

Valerie Cass looked rather piqued, but replied, "No, I expect he's sorting out the details of the transfer."

So she still believed in it. Presumably, her daughter did, too. It would be in keeping with her habitual breathless optimism.

He didn't know whether to disillusion Valerie or not, but the decision was taken away from him by the arrival of Paul Lexington.

The cast drew apart to make room for him, drew apart with respect or loathing, as if uncertain whether they were dealing with royalty or with a leper. It all really depended on what news he bore.

Paul Lexington seemed aware of this as he clapped his hands for silence.

"Ladies and gentlemen, I'd like to thank you all for all the hard work you've put into making *The Hooded Owl* such a great success in Taunton . . ."

The silence was almost tangible. Was that all he had to say? Was that it? Was Taunton the end?

The producer looked absolutely exhausted, but seemed almost to be playing with them, timing his lines to maximise the suspense.

"And I would like to say," he continued after a long pause, "that today I have finally persuaded Bobby Anscombe to come into partnership with me to transfer the production to the West End! *The Hooded Owl* will open at the Variety Theatre on 30th October!"

The last sentence was lost in the cast's screams of delight. Everyone leapt about, hugging each other, laughing, crying, howling with relief.

Charles Paris joined in the celebration, but he felt a slight detachment, a reserve within him. Because of the conversation he had overheard, Paul Lexington's words did not quite ring true. The producer had had Bobby Anscombe's assent a full week before.

Sure, there must have been details to sort out, but Charles couldn't lose the feeling that Paul Lexington had deliberately prolonged the cast's agony for reasons of his own.

What reasons? Hard to say. Maybe just to delay sorting out contracts for the West End, to avoid paying an extra week's retainer or rehearsal money . . .

Charles regretted his suspicions, and tried to convince himself that they were unworthy. But he couldn't. After the fast one Paul Lexington had pulled on Malcolm Harris, it was going to be a long time before he regained the trust of Charles Paris.

CHAPTER FOUR

"HELLO, FRANCES, it's me."

"Charles! Where are you? How are you?"

"I'm in London and I'm fine."

"I'm so glad you rang. There are things I need to talk to you about."

"That sounds ominous."

"Not too ominous. Just business."

"Business is by definition ominous. Still, if you want to talk to me, I would like to talk to you. Can I take you out to dinner tonight?"

"Oh, Charles . . . I'm meant to be doing some marking."

"I thought when you were headmistress you delegated such menial tasks as marking."

"Don't you believe it."

"Oh, come on. A quick dinner with me and then you can do the marking when you get back."

"I know quick dinners with you, Charles. You'll get me back late and too drunk to read the stuff, let alone mark it."

"Oh, Frances . . . I am your husband. Don't I have any rights to your time?"

Shouldn't have said that. Not a very good argument, as Frances was quick to point out. Rather frostily.

"I think you've allowed any claims you might have on my time to lapse for too long, Charles."

"O.K., forget I said that. Just come out to dinner with me for the pleasure of coming out to dinner with me."

There was a silence from the other end of the line. Then she gave in. "All right. It'd be good to see you. But, by the way, what is all this inviting ladies out to dinner? Not your usual style. Have you won the pools or something?"

"Better than that, dear. I'm just about to star in a West End show."

"Are you? Well, in that case, I'll expect a big bunch of red roses too."

37

He arrived at the Hampstead bistro first (almost unprecedented), with a big bunch of red roses (totally unprecedented), and asked the waiter for a vase to put them in. He then hid behind the foliage, and waited.

The expression on Frances's face when she saw the flowers showed what a good idea they had been. He was always slightly amazed at how effective such corny old gestures were, and surprised that he didn't resort to them more often.

"Charles, how sweet of you."

"And how spontaneous," he said wryly as he kissed her.

She sat down and saw the glass of white wine he had ordered for her. "You even remembered what I drink. You're in danger of becoming a smoothie, Charles Paris."

"Really?" He was drawn to the idea.

"No, not really. There's no danger so long as you keep that sports jacket. Cheers."

They clinked glasses and drank.

"So what's this West End thing?"

"Well, you know the play I've just been doing down at Taunton . . . ?"

"No."

"But I thought I—"

"Charles, it's three months since you've been in touch."

"Oh, is it?" Putting that behind him, he pressed on. "Well, I've just been doing a play at the Prince's Theatre, Taunton, thing called *The Hooded Owl*, and, quite simply, it's coming in!"

"That's terrific. Have you got a good part?"

He smiled complacently. "Not bad."

"So when do you open?"

"Thursday, 30th October. We have this week free—well, there's a meeting on Friday to sort out rehearsal schedules and what-have-you —then start rerehearsals on Monday, two weeks of polishing it up, three previews from the 27th—and then the grand opening, which will of course make my fortune, so that, in the evening of my life, I become a grand old man of the British Thea-taaah."

The irony of his tone was very familiar to her. "Don't you be so cynical, Charles Paris. Why shouldn't it work?"

"I have been here a few times before."

"And this may be the time that it really takes off."

"Maybe." And he couldn't help grinning as she voiced his secret dream.

He told her more about the play and then asked about his daughter, Juliet.

"Oh, she's fine. And Miles. And the twins."

Of course. Juliet didn't really exist on her own any more. It was Juliet and husband Miles, who was in insurance and, to Charles's mind, without doubt the most boring man in the world. Not only Miles, but also the twins, their lives already blighted, in their grandfather's view, by having been christened Julian and Damian.

"How old are they now?"

"They were four in April. I sent them presents from both of us."

"Ah," said Charles awkwardly. "Thank you."

"I wouldn't be surprised if Juliet didn't start another one soon."

"Another what?"

"Baby."

"Oh."

So Miles reckoned the international financial scene could cope with another child. Hmm, maybe the recession was bottoming out.

"They'd love to see you."

"Sure, I'd love to see them," he replied automatically. "Incidentally—apropos of Miles—you said there was something boring you wanted to talk to me about."

Frances grinned guiltily. "You must stop saying things like that about Miles."

"Why? It's true. Or have I missed something? Go on, tell me, I'm anxious to know—have you ever heard an interesting word pass our son-in-law's lips?"

"I decline to answer that. Juliet's very happy with him."

"Thank you. You have answered it."

"Anyway," said Frances, heavily changing the subject, "what I wanted to talk to you about was the house."

"Our house in Muswell Hill?"

"Yes. I want to sell it."

"Sell it?"

"And move in somewhere smaller."

"Are you hard up?"

"No, I'm better off than ever now I'm headmistress. But I'm also busier, and a house like that takes a lot of time."

"I suppose it does. I'd never really thought about it."

"And I'm over fifty now and have to start looking ahead to retirement. So selling the house seems the logical thing to do."

"Hmm."

"You don't mind, do you?"

"Mind? No, why should I mind?"

But he did. Somehow, through all the extravagations of his life, he still thought of Frances in the house in Muswell Hill as a fixed point, a moral and geographical norm from which everything else was a kind of deviation. He was surprised at the emptiness he felt at the prospect of her moving. That sort of thing, like Juliet thinking of having another baby, like the twins growing up, made him feel abandoned, immobile in a world where everything else was on the move.

He tried not to show his hurt, because he knew he had no justification for it, but for him the sparkle had gone out of the rest of the meal.

He saw Frances to her car, a bright yellow Renault 5, another symbol of her independence of him.

"Shall I . . . er . . ?"

"No, Charles. I've got to do that marking."

"Sure."

She thanked him for a lovely evening and for the roses, with a strange formality, almost as if they had just met for the first time.

"We'll meet up again soon," he said.

"Yes, I'd love that."

She kissed him gently on the lips and was gone.

Charles found a cab and gave the driver the address of the Montrose, a drinking club off the Haymarket.

"Hello, Maurice Skellern Personal Management."

"Maurice, it's me, Charles."

"Oh, hello."

"What's with all this 'Personal Management'? I thought you were called 'Maurice Skellern Artistes'."

"Yes, I was, Charles, but I decided it had a rather dated feel. 'Artistes' is so . . . I don't know . . . so *Variety*. I thought 'Personal Management' had a more with-it, seventies feel."

"We're in the eighties, Maurice."

"Oh yes, so we are. Well, you know what I mean."

"Hmm. In my experience, 'Personal Management' usually means the agent taking twenty per cent rather than ten."

"Ah yes, well, Charles, we must talk about that sometime. Anyway, how did the play go down in Bristol?"

"Taunton."

40

"Taunton, Bristol—it's all West Country. Anyway, how was it?"

"You mean you haven't heard?"

"Heard what?"

"Honestly, Maurice! I thought agents were meant to be the antennae of show business, alert to every rumour, every flicker of interest. I don't think you even know where the West End is."

"You know, Charles, sometimes you can be very hurtful."

"Listen. *The Hooded Owl* was a very big success in Taunton."

"Oh, good."

"And it's coming in to the West End."

"REALLY?"

"Yes. Opening on 30th October at the Varietyoh."

"What's the Varietyoh?"

"The Variety. It just saves you the trouble of saying 'oh' in a disappointed voice."

"Oh," said Maurice, in a disappointed voice.

"No, it'll be all right. Denis Thornton's got the lease of the theatre now."

"Has he?"

"And Bobby Anscombe's backing the show."

"IS HE?"

"Yes, I'm surprised you haven't heard anything about it."

"Now, Charles, I'm not as young as I was. I don't get about the way I—"

"No, I meant I was surprised the management hadn't been in touch to sort out the West End contract. You sure you haven't heard anything?"

"Not a squeak."

"Oh well, they must be pretty busy this week. There's a meeting tomorrow. No doubt I'll hear more then."

"Yes. You don't want me to ring anyone?" asked Maurice, with distaste at the prospect.

"No, don't bother."

"You know, Charles, this is very good news. Very good news. It's really gratifying for me, you know, as an agent . . ."

"Oh yes?"

"Yes, when one feels that all one's hard work has not been in vain, that all that careful guiding of a client's career has not been wasted. Yes, moments like this make one understand the meaning of Personal Management."

"Oh yes?"

"Now, Charles, about this rate of commission you pay me . . ."

The Friday's meeting for the company of *The Hooded Owl* was held in a superannuated gym near Covent Garden. Everyone was in good spirits, ranging from the quiet complacency of Alex Household to the Christmas Eve child's exhilaration of Lesley-Jane Decker. The week's break had relaxed them with that relaxation an actor can only feel when he knows he's got a job to go to. Those based on London had seen friends, seen shows, talked endlessly; those based outside had sorted out digs or friends to land themselves on, seen shows, talked endlessly. And when they all met up again in the gym, they talked further, volubly, dramatically, hysterically.

The meeting was called for three in the afternoon, but by three-fifteen there was still no sign of Paul Lexington. At one end of the gym there was a folding table with a couple of chairs, from which he would no doubt address them when he arrived. One chair was already occupied by a young man in a beige suit with immaculately waved hair. No one knew who he was or made any attempt to talk to him, but he didn't seem worried by this. He just sat at the table looking through some papers and playing with a pencil.

Peter Hickton wasn't expected at the meeting. He was still monitoring his next Taunton production, *Ten Little Indians* (called by its author, Agatha Christie, in less sensitive times, *Ten Little Niggers*), which had opened on the Wednesday. He would come up to town for the rerehearsal, starting on the following Monday. In the view of most of the cast, two weeks was an excessive allocation of time to rerehearse a show they had brought to such a pitch of perfection in Taunton. They reckoned they were in for a fairly lazy fortnight.

At three-twenty Paul Lexington arrived. He clutched a brief-case full of papers, and still looked pretty exhausted, but he had lost the wild look of the last week at Taunton. His confidence had returned a hundredfold.

"Sorry I'm late, everyone. There's been a lot to arrange, and one particular deal I only got signed half an hour ago. Have you all met Wallas?"

He indicated the young man in the beige suit. No, it was clear no one had met him. "Ah, this is Wallas Ward, who is going to be our Company Manager."

Wallas Ward nodded languidly, and the company looked at him with new interest. The Company Manager would play a significant part in their lives during the run. He was the management's representative, responsible for the day-to-day running of the show. It would help if the cast got on with him, though, because of his allegiance to the management, they would never quite trust him.

"Right," said Paul. "I'm sorry that we haven't got round to contacting your agents during the last week, but it has been very busy. I've had to set up a Production Office, sort out the deals with Denis Thornton and Bobby Anscombe—there's been a hell of a lot to do.

"Still, the important bits are now settled, and the result of it all is . . ." He paused, seeming uncertain, which was out of character for him. "Well, let me say that I have some good news and some bad news for you."

The cast was absolutely silent. This was the first discordant note since the euphoria of the Taunton party.

"Now, as you know, Bobby Anscombe is coming in with me on this production. The credit'll read: 'Paul Lexington Productions, in association with Bobby Anscombe'. Now this is excellent news for the show. I don't think I need to give you a list of Bobby's successes. He's got the best nose in the business, and the fact that he's with us means that we're going to have a hit . . ."

He paused again. The cast still hardly breathed. They hadn't had the bad news yet.

Paul Lexington chose his words with care. "Now Bobby Anscombe's success in the theatre hasn't been just coincidence. He knows what makes a show work, and, if all the elements aren't there, he has never been sentimental about making changes as necessary."

There was a tiny rustle of unease from the cast. They were beginning to anticipate what was coming.

"Now I think it's no secret from any of you that when we opened the play in Taunton, we were hoping to have a star name in the cast."

They all knew now. Imperceptibly, they all glanced towards Salome Search, whose face shone with tension.

"We didn't get a star name, but we got an excellent performance, and the show was still a huge success. And, for myself, I'd like to keep that success intact. I don't believe in changing a winning team.

"However . . ."

Moisture glowed on Salome Search's eyes.

"Bobby Anscombe does not agree with me. Obviously he's more objective than I am, he doesn't know you all, he hasn't worked with you all. But his view is that to bring in a play by an unknown author *without any star names* is commercial suicide. He wants to make changes in the cast.

"Now I've argued with him about this, but he won't budge. In fact, what it comes down to is, if we don't make cast changes, he'll back out. I've checked round other potential investors and there's nothing doing. Either we do the show with Bobby Anscombe—or the transfer's off."

The cast was once again silent.

"I'm sorry I have to break the news to you like this. I'd rather have spoken quietly to the individuals concerned, but I'm afraid there hasn't been time. So I'm going to be brutal and just tell you . . ."

He paused. Once again, as at the cast party, Charles wondered whether the producer wasn't rather enjoying the suspense he created. There seemed to be a kind of glee behind the apology, a relish in the role of hatchet-man.

"Alex," Paul Lexington announced finally, "I am afraid you're out. We've just done a deal with Micky Banks to play the part of the father."

Now at last he got reaction, but it was a confused reaction. If he hadn't mentioned the name of the replacement, the cast would have been shouting at him in fury, in defence of the one of them who had been so savagely axed. But Michael Banks . . . Even in their moment of shock, they could recognise what a coup it was to get him. Now if ever a name was box office, it was Micky Banks. And though their hearts went out to Alex, their actor's fickleness could appreciate the commercial sense of substitution.

Alex Household himself was the slowest to react. The noise around him subsided and they all looked covertly towards him.

"I see," he said, very, very coolly.

"I'm sorry," said the producer. "If it could have happened any other way, I'd've . . . I'm sure we can sort out some sort of deal for you. I mean of course, you haven't signed any sort of contract . . ."

I see, thought Charles. Maybe that was the reason for delaying the announcement of the transfer; maybe that was why no approach had been made to any of their agents. Paul Lexington hadn't wanted to get any of the original cast signed up until he had contracted his star.

"But I'm sure, Alex, we can sort out some sort of generous terms for you if you want to understudy—"

"Understudy!" the actor repeated, rising to his feet. "Under-study . . ."

"I mean it's up to you. You just say what you want and I'll—"

"Say what I want, eh?" Alex's anger was beginning to build. "Say

44

what I want. Shall I tell you what I want? I want the world rid of all the little shits like you who run it. I want you all out—gone—dead—exterminated!"

"Look, Alex, I'm sorry—"

"Sorry, yes, but you're not as sorry as you will be! You dare to offer me the job of understudy to a part I CREATED! Well, you know what you can do with your job—stuff it! Understudy!"

And, with that sense of occasion that never deserts an actor even in the most real crises of emotion, Alex Household exited from the gym.

There was a murmur of mixed reaction from the cast. They were sorry, yes, angry, yes, but inside each felt relief. In each mind was the same thought: It wasn't *me*.

"I'm sorry, this is very painful," Paul Lexington continued, with the same hint of relish. "It's not the part of the producer's job that I enjoy.

"I mentioned cast chan*ges*."

They were all struck dumb again. In their relief they had forgotten that. The axe was still poised overhead. Eyes again slid round to Salome Search.

"Charles," said Paul Lexington, "I'm sorry . . ."

CHAPTER FIVE

CHARLES WAS no less hurt than Alex Household at losing his part in *The Hooded Owl*, but his way of showing the hurt was different. He was not quick to anger and confrontation; shocks caught up with him slowly and he usually faced them in solitary depression rather than by throwing a scene. A bottle of Bell's was the only witness of his lowest moods.

It was just the two of them. The rest of the cast had survived the axe. Charles stayed at the meeting long enough to hear when the rehearsal call was for the Monday; if he accepted Paul's offer of an understudy job, then he'd have to be there. But he wasn't sure whether he was going to accept. He said he'd think about it over the weekend, and let Paul know on the Monday.

When he left, the other actors offered him clumsy commiseration, as to someone who had been bereaved. And, as to the bereaved, their words glowed with the grateful confidence that their own worlds were still intact.

It was when he got outside into the sunlight of a newly-trendy Covent Garden that the disappointment hit him. His armour of cynicism was shown up as useless; all he could feel was how desperately he had wanted the job and how bitter he felt at the injustice that had taken it away from him.

Because it was injustice; he knew it wasn't a matter of talent. He had played that part well, certainly at least as well as the actor who was to take over from him.

George Birkitt.

He knew George Birkitt, had worked with him on a television sit. com. called *The Strutters*. He liked George Birkitt and thought he was a good actor. But to lose the part to George Birkitt . . . that he found hard to stomach.

And why? Simply because George Birkitt was a better-known name from television. After *The Strutters*, he had gone on to play a leading

46

part in another sit. com. called *Fly-Buttons*. That had just started screening as part of the ITV Autumn Season and so suddenly George Birkitt was a familiar name. The sort of name which, on a poster—particularly if placed directly beneath that of Michael Banks—would in theory bring the punters in.

Whereas Charles Paris, who knew that he had given one of the best performances of his career in *The Hooded Owl*, was a name that the punters wouldn't know from a bar of soap.

So he was out, and George Birkitt was in.

Charles just walked. Walked through the streets of London. He often did at times of emotional crisis. He didn't really notice where he was going, just plodded on mechanically.

The sight of an open pub told him how much time had passed and also reminded him of his normal comfort in moments of stress.

But he didn't want to sit in a pub, listening to the jollity and in-jokes of office workers.

He went into an off-licence and bought a large bottle of Bell's.

But he didn't want just to go back to Hereford Road and drink it on his own.

He needed someone to talk to. Someone who would understand what he was going through.

There was only one person who would really understand, because he was going through exactly the same. And that was Alex Household.

The new flat was at the top of a tall house in Bloomsbury, round the back of the British Museum. Alex opened the door suspiciously and, when he saw who was there, was about to shut it again.

"I don't want your bloody sympathy, Charles!"

"That's not what I'm bringing. I've got the boot too."

"Oh Lord." Alex Household drew aside to let him into the flat. The interior was still full of boxes and packing cases, showing signs of recent occupation.

"I've bought a bottle of whisky and I'm planning to drink my way right through it." Charles slumped on to a sofa. "You going to help me, or are you still on the 'no stimulants' routine?"

"I'll help you. What does it matter what I do now?"

"Transcendental meditation no good? Doesn't the 'earth's plenty'—"

"Listen, Charles!" Alex turned in fury, his fist clenched.

"Sorry. Stupid remark. I'm as screwed up as you are."

"Yes, I must say this is a wonderful 'new start'." Alex laughed bitterly. "For the last few months I've really been feeling together, an integrated personality for the first time since my breakdown. And now . . . Do you know, my psychiatrist spent hour after hour convincing me that it was all in the mind, that nobody really was out to get me, that the world wasn't conspiring against me . . . And I'd just about begun to believe him. And now—this. Something like this happens and you realise it's all true. The world really is conspiring against you. I'd like to see a psychiatrist convince me this is all in the mind. It's a—"

Charles interrupted him crudely. "Glasses. Be too sordid for both of us to drink out of the bottle."

Alex went off for glasses and Charles put the bottle down on a coffee table. As he did so, he moved a handkerchief that was lying on it.

He uncovered a gun. The Smith and Wesson Chiefs Special.

Alex saw him looking at it as he came back with the glasses. "Yes, I'd just got that out when you rang the bell."

"Thinking of using it?"

Alex smiled a little twisted smile. "Had crossed my mind. Trouble was, I couldn't decide whether to use it on myself or on the rest of the bastards."

Charles laughed uneasily. "I'm sure your psychiatrist wouldn't recommend suicide."

"No, he wouldn't. He was a great believer in *expressing* aggression, not bottling it up. If I were to take this gun and shoot . . . who? Paul Lexington? Micky Banks? Bobby Anscombe? Doesn't matter, there are so many of them. No, if I were to do that, my psychiatrist would reckon it proved my cure was complete." He suddenly found this notion very funny and burst into laughter.

Charles poured two large measures of Bell's and handed one over. The laughter subsided, leaving Alex drained and depressed.

"So what are you going to do, Alex?"

"What do you mean?"

"About the understudy job."

"I don't know," the actor intoned lethargically. "It'd be work, I suppose. I could keep on the flat."

"And see Lesley-Jane . . ."

"Yes." The name evinced no sign of interest. "Give me another drink."

Charles obliged, and filled up his own at the same time.

"Were you offered the same deal, Charles?"

"What—the great honour of understudying my own part? Oh yes, Paul nobly offered me that."

"And what are you going to do about it?"

"God knows. Ask my agent, I suppose."

"Hmm. Give me another drink."

"Maurice, it's Charles."

"I wish you wouldn't ring me at home. I try to keep work and my private life separate."

"I know, but this is important. And it's the weekend."

"You don't have to tell me that, Charles."

"Was that your wife I spoke to?"

"Mind your own business."

"Listen, Maurice, about *The Hooded Owl* . . . I've got the boot."

"Yes, I know."

"Oh, all of a sudden you know. On Thursday you didn't even know the show was transferring."

"No, I had a call yesterday afternoon from Paul . . . Leamington?'

"Lexington."

"Yes. Pleasant young man he sounded."

"Oh, a great charmer."

"Anyway, he told me about the necessity of recasting. And I said, of course, I fully understood."

"Thank you very much."

"Now what's that tone of voice for, Charles?"

"Well, really! You 'fully understood' that your client had got the sack. Why didn't you stand up for me?"

"Now come on, Charles. We both know you're a very good actor, but you're not a *name*, are you?"

"Hardly surprising, with you for a bloody agent," Charles mumbled.

"What was that, Charles? I didn't catch it."

"Never mind."

"Well, anyway, the good news is that Mr. Leventon—"

"Lexington."

"Yes, has offered most attractive terms for an understudy contract for you."

"Oh, terrific."

"No, really very generous. I mean, a hundred and fifty a week—that's as much as I'd've expected you to get for actually *acting*."

Blood money, thought Charles.

49

"Six-month contract, too. I mean, when were you last offered a six-month contract for anything?"

"So you reckon I should take it?"

"Well, of course, Charles. What's the alternative?"

"No other lucrative jobs on the horizon?"

"'Fraid not, Charles. As you know, it's not a good time. All the provincial companies have sorted out their seasons, most of the big tellies are cast, there's not much on the—"

"Yes, all right, all right. In other words, things are exactly as usual."

"Yes."

"And you really think I should take it?"

"Yes. I can't think why you're havering. It's obvious. A very good offer."

"Yes, but it is understudying a part I've already played—and played well."

"So?"

"So . . . it becomes a matter of pride."

"Pride? You, Charles? Oh, really." And Maurice Skellern let out a gasping laugh, as if the joke had really cheered up his weekend.

It was inevitable that, when rerehearsals started on the Monday, the centre of attention should be Michael Banks. His theatrical successes exceeded those of all the rest of the cast added together (and the money Paul Lexington had agreed with his agent quite possibly exceeded their total too).

His face was so familiar that he seemed to have been with the production for weeks. Few of the cast would have seen him in the revues of the late thirties where his career started, but they would all have caught up with the films he had made in the immediate post-war years. He had had a distinguished war, being wounded once and decorated twice, and had spent the next five years recreating it in a series of patriotic British movies. Michael Banks it always was who gazed grimly at the enemy submarine from the bridge, Michael Banks who went back for the wounded private in the jungle, Michael Banks who ignored the smoke pouring from his Spitfire's engine as he trained his sights on the alien Messerschmidt.

He had then gone to Hollywood in the early fifties and stayed there long enough to show that he could cope with the system and be moderately successful, but not so long as to alienate his chauvinistic British following.

The West End then beckoned, and he appeared as a solid juvenile in a sequence of light comedies. He was good box office and managements fell over themselves to get his name on their marquees.

That continued until the early sixties, when, for the first time, his career seemed to be under threat. Fashions had changed; the new youth-oriented culture had nothing but contempt for the gritty, laconic heroism of the war, of which Michael Banks remained the symbol. The trendies of Carnaby Street flounced around in military uniforms, sporting flowers of peace where medals once had hung. Acting styles changed too, as did the plays in which they were exhibited. The mannered delivery of West End comedies sounded ridiculous at the kitchen sink, and became the butt of the booming satire industry.

"The wind of change", that phrase coined by Harold Macmillan in 1960, grew to have a more general application than just to Africa, or just to politics. It represented a change of style, and this new wind threatened to blow away all that was dated and traditional.

Amongst other things, it threatened to blow away the career of Michael Banks.

And it might well have done. He had reached that most difficult of ages for a successful actor, his forties. The audience who had loved him as a stage juvenile were themselves growing old, and could not fail to notice the signs of ageing in their idol. The rising generation was not interested. To them Michael Banks represented that anathema—something their parents liked. If they saw him in a play, they saw a middle-aged man pretending to be young, in an outdated vehicle that bore as much relation to their reality as crinolines and penny-farthings.

He did two more West End comedies, neither of which lasted three months, and theatre managements were suddenly less anxious to pick up the phone and plead with his agent. The British film industry, such as it was, was committed to making zany films about Swinging London and, if there were any parts for the over-forties, they went to outrageous character actors.

One or two offers of touring productions or guest star status in provincial reps came in, a sure sign that their managements were trying to cash in on the name of Michael Banks before it was completely forgotten.

It was the nadir of his career. He was all right financially—he had always been shrewd and he had made his money in days when the Inland Revenue had allowed people to keep some of it—but his prospects of regaining his former place in the public's esteem seemed negligible.

51

The way he had fought back from that position showed that the grit demonstrated in all those celluloid heroics was not just acting. He had survived by sheer determination.

His first decision had been only to take on older parts. He refused every sort of juvenile role that was offered, resisting lucrative inducements to recreate his West End successes in the diminished settings of the provinces or seasons in South Africa and Australia.

The result of this policy change was a very quiet three years. He played one Blimpish cameo in a short-lived play in Birmingham and a couple of small parts in television plays.

It wasn't an enjoyable period of his life, but he stuck it out, certain that he was on the right track. He deliberately courted very old parts, particularly on television. He realised the medium's power, and realised that, through it, he could reach a different public and establish a new image with them. The West End and even cinema audiences were tiny compared to the huge passive mass of armchair viewers. He reasoned that, if he could establish a new, older identity with them, he would be able to shake off the persona of faded juvenile.

Age was not the only criterion in his choice of parts. He avoided the trendy and the experimental, aiming ideally for costume drama, aware that his strengths were those of permanence and reliability, and would be dissipated by following the twists of fashion. And he had a gut-feeling that the values of that huge but silent force, the British middle class, were the same as his own. The television-viewing public was made up of the older stay-at-homes, not the swinging exotics whose exploits filled the front pages of the newspapers. They might not dare to admit it, but they didn't like the changes they saw around them; they enjoyed television's recreations of more confident times, when they had had a country to be proud of, when people had reached maturity at forty and had not pandered to youth. They liked seeing the old values reasserted.

And, gradually, through the parts he chose, Michael Banks came to symbolise those values.

His three years in the wilderness climaxed with a solid part in a BBC costume drama series. It was not the lead, but the character was in every episode, and had the advantage of ageing from week to week.

The public took the character to their hearts. Once again, they took Michael Banks to their hearts. Having watched him grow old before their eyes in their own sitting-rooms, they would thereafter accept him in parts of any age.

Since that time, his career had had no more problems. He had become increasingly selective in what he did, avoiding, on the whole, long runs in the West End, and concentrating on starring television parts or extremely lucrative cameos in international films. He became an institution of British acting, respected and loved. In the business, you never heard a word against Michael Banks.

And, when the cast of *The Hooded Owl* met him, they could understand why. He was an immensely likeable man. He was in his sixties, but had aged gracefully. The familiar acute face had thickened out, and the hair, remembered as darker than it actually was because of all those black-and-white films, had greyed becomingly. It was cut in a trendier style, worn longer than it would have been, but its shape still reminded one of all those gruff but infinitely reliable heroes. He dressed casually in a red golfing sweater, pale blue trousers, and deceptively ordinary-looking hand-made shoes.

The surprise about him was his size. As actors, they were all used to people looking different off screen, but none of them had expected him to be so tall. He must have been six foot four, with a frame to match. A most impressive figure. The reasoning behind casting him as the father in *The Hooded Owl* became clearer by the minute.

Clearer to Charles, anyway. He was at the rehearsal, needless to say, having, possibly for the first time in his life, followed his agent's advice. Through the haze of Bell's which had been the weekend, it had become clear that he had little alternative. He was being offered a job, being offered good money, and he'd be based in London. His dreams would have to wait, be returned intact to some cupboard deep in the recesses of his mind, whence they would arise, undaunted, at the next glimmer of hope in his career.

To his surprise, the strongest argument in favour of taking the job had been that it would keep him near to Frances. Her talk of moving, and the indefinable detachment he had felt in her when they had met, worried him. He felt he needed to rebuild the relationship—not, of course, to revive it as a total marriage, but to get back to the level of intermittent companionship which seemed to have gone.

Similar arguments must have weighed with Alex Household, because he was there too. His face looked strained and petulant, but he had clearly decided to put his mortgage and proximity to Lesley-Jane above pride.

If the cast had needed a demonstration of Michael Banks's genuine warmth, they could not have asked for a better one than the way he dealt with Alex Household.

The first thing he did on arriving at the rehearsal room was to ask Paul Lexington which one was Alex and, having had him identified, he immediately went across to the actor with hand outstretched.

"Alex, I'm sorry. This is a lousy way for me to get a job. I know exactly how you feel. Just the same thing happened to me on one of my first jobs. It was a revue back in the thirties. We were doing a pre-London tour. I got as far as Birmingham, and then was called into the manager's office. Just the same as you, I was offered the understudy."

"Did you take it?"

"Oh yes." Michael Banks grinned disarmingly. "Oh yes, I took it. And it does mean I know exactly how shitty you're feeling at this moment, and all the horrible fates you're wishing down on my head."

Alex blushed. "Oh, I wouldn't say . . ."

"Yes, you would. You wouldn't be human if you didn't. Anyway, all I want to say is—I'm very sorry. This can be a rotten business at times. I sympathise. And, if you're willing, I'll be very grateful for your help. God, you must know this character inside-out by now, and I've got to get it presentable in a fortnight. Any tips you can give me, old boy, I will welcome as rich gifts."

It was beautifully done. Had it been less well done, someone as prickly and paranoid as Alex Household would have bridled, would have pointed out that to lose a part at the beginning of one's career was rather different from losing it after twenty years in the business, would have made some bitter retort. But, as it was, Michael Banks had him eating out of his hand. Yes, of course, said Alex, no, he couldn't pretend he wasn't hurt, but thanks for saying it, and he'd be happy to give any advice that might be required.

George Birkitt didn't show quite the same smooth tact in his dealings with the actor he was replacing.

"Hello, Charles. Long time, no see," he murmured after getting himself a coffee.

"Hello."

"Rather strange circumstances for a meeting."

"Yes."

"I was very undecided when my agent told me about the offer . . ."

"Oh."

"Well, it *is* second billing, no two ways about that. I mean, God knows, I'm the last person in the world to worry about that sort of thing, but there does come a point in your career where you *have* to think about it. I mean, with *Fly-Buttons* up there in the ratings, I do have to be a bit careful." He lowered his voice. "I tell you, Charles, it was only after I heard that they'd signed up Micky Banks that I agreed to do it. Of course, it *is* still second billing, but second billing to Micky Banks is no disgrace at this stage in my career."

"No, I suppose not," said Charles.

Peter Hickton was up from Taunton and keen to start working his cast as hard as ever. Now that the two main parts had been recast, there really was going to be a lot to do, and the company waved goodbye to their hopes of a cushy fortnight.

The director clapped his hands. "O.K., loves. Now, as you all know, we've got a big job on, and we're going to have to work every hour there is to get *The Hooded Owl* up to the standard I know it can reach."

This was very familiar to those who had worked with Peter before; he said it before every production, regardless of how complex or simple it was, and regardless of the length of rehearsal allocated.

"Now what I want to do is go through the blocking today, so that Micky and George can start to feel the shape of the production. Tomorrow we'll get down to Act One in detail, and then on Wednesday we'll—"

"Um, sorry, old boy . . ."

Peter Hickton looked to the source of the interruption. It was Michael Banks.

"Yes?"

"Sorry, can't do Wednesday."

"What?"

"Can't do Wednesday. Got to do some Pro-Celebrity Golf thing for the BBC. Didn't the agent mention it?"

Peter Hickton looked round to Paul Lexington, who shook his head.

"Oh, I'm so sorry. The agent's an awful duffer when it comes to dates. Got the same thing the following Wednesday too."

"Oh." But Peter Hickton was only slowed down for a moment. "Never mind. If we work hard over the weekend, we can—"

"Ah. Sorry, old boy, going away for the weekend."

"Oh."

"Going to stay with some chums in Chichester. Can't really put it off, been in the diary for ages. Sorry, this show came up so suddenly, there are a few dates we'll have to work round."

"Yes," said Peter Hickton. "Yes, of course."

55

Under normal circumstances, understudies would be expected to attend all the rehearsals to familiarise themselves with the production, but, because Alex and Charles knew the play so well, they were given a dispensation to take most of the first week off, which would save both them and their replacements the embarrassment of the early stumbling rehearsals while the newcomers were trying to memorise the lines. The two understudies were asked to come back on the Friday afternoon, when there was going to be a complete run of the play for the producers and Malcolm Harris.

When he arrived at the rehearsal room on the Friday, Charles found the author in a state of extreme annoyance.

"What's up, Malcolm?"

"Have you seen this?" He pointed to a printed handout on a table. It read:

THE VARIETY THEATRE
PAUL LEXINGTON PRODUCTIONS
in association with
BOBBY ANSCOMBE
presents
MICHAEL BANKS
GEORGE BIRKITT
in

THE HOODED OWL

There was more writing beneath this, but it was printed too small to be legible.

"I see," said Charles.

"It's a bit much. My name might just as well not be on it," objected the author.

"Hmm. You see, what's happened is that this is a big design for a poster. They've economised by reducing it for the handout. Your name'd be legible on the big poster."

"That's a fat lot of good. No, I'm really annoyed about this. I think these handouts should be withdrawn. I mean, look at the size of Paul's name—it's as big as Michael Banks, for God's sake."

"Producer's perk. He decides what the poster looks like."

"Well, I'm furious. Who should I complain to about it?"

"Under normal circumstances," said Charles gently, "you'd go to your agent and get him to complain to the management."

"Ah," said Malcolm Harris, realising, perhaps for the first time, the folly of the contract he had signed with Paul Lexington.

"Good news about getting Michael Banks, isn't it?" said Charles, to cheer up the hangdog author.

It had the desired effect. Malcolm Harris brightened immediately. "Yes, it's wonderful. From the moment I first thought of the play, I thought he'd be ideal for the part. Though, of course, I never dared hope . . ."

The run-through started. Charles could not judge George Birkitt's performance, he was too close to the part to be objective, but there was no doubt that Michael Banks was going to be very strong as the father. In his first scene he established an unshakeable authority, which, Charles knew, was bound to strengthen the total collapse of the character in the second act. Alex Household had been excellent in the part, but, in retrospect, he seemed to have been giving an actor's interpretation of a man fifteen years older than himself. Michael Banks actually seemed to *be* that man.

But, after the first scene, the performance weakened. The power of the acting remained, but its flow was constantly interrupted. The actor just did not know the lines, and, though he could manage the exchanges of dialogue quite well, every time he came to a big speech, he would dry.

"Sorry, old boy. Sorry, loves. Prompt," he would say. The Stage Manager would give him the line, he'd be all right for a couple more sentences, then, "Sorry, it's gone again."

The play tottered on like this for a quarter of an hour. Charles was sitting at the back of the hall with Malcolm Harris, and kept feeling the author tense as another of his speeches was chopped up and destroyed. Eventually, Michael Banks just stopped, looked out at the director, and said, "Look, sorry, Peter old boy, I'd better use the book. Not getting anywhere like this."

"I did want to do this run without books."

"So did I, dear boy, so did I," said the star lugubriously, and got a good laugh from the cast. He had managed to endear himself to all of them within the week, and they shared his agony as he groped for the lines.

"We open in less than a fortnight," Peter Hickton continued to argue.

"Don't think I don't know it. But, honestly, I think we'll just be wasting time if I go on like this."

"You've got to come off the book sometime."

"I will, I will, love. I promise. Look, don't worry about it. I'm usually pretty good on lines. Once, when I was in rep, I learned Iago in three days. So it will come, just hasn't come yet. So I think for this run I'd better press on with the book."

Michael Banks's charm didn't prevent him from being forceful, and Peter Hickton had to concede defeat. The play continued. With the support of the printed lines, Michael Banks's performance regained the stature it had shown in the first scene and left no doubt that he was going to add a new excellence to *The Hooded Owl*. Charles found he was watching much of the play as if seeing it for the first time.

Towards the end of the second act, the door beside him opened and a woman slipped in to the back of the hall. She was in her forties, smartly dressed in white trousers, *eau-de-nil* silk shirt and long camel-coloured cardigan. Very well-preserved. She flashed a well-crowned smile at Charles.

"Hi," she whispered. "I'm Dottie, Micky's wife."

"Charles Paris."

"How's it going?"

"Pretty good."

She nodded and her alert hazel eyes flickered around the room, taking everyone in. They lingered on Lesley-Jane Decker. "Who's that?" she hissed.

Charles gave the girl's name.

"Micky made a play for her yet?"

He was surprised. "I don't know. I haven't been round much this week." Then, curious, "Why? Has he got a roving eye?"

"Haven't we all?" she said. Her tone was mocking, but she was fully aware of the sexual nature of her remark.

The play ended. Malcolm Harris started to applaud and some of the others joined in. Michael Banks grinned and went across to have a word with Lesley-Jane. After Dottie's remark, Charles couldn't help thinking that the two of them did look rather intimate.

Peter Hickton clapped his hands again. "O.K., thank you all very much. We really are getting somewhere. There are a few scenes I'd just like to run through before we break and—"

"Sorry, love," said Michael Banks gently. "Got to go. Off for the weekend, as I said, old boy." He waved vaguely to Dottie.

"But I really think we should—" the director began.

"Sorry. No can do."

"Are you sure you can't just stay for—"

58

Michael Banks shook his head charmingly. "Sorry, love."

"Oh. Oh, well . . . You will have a look at the lines over the week-end, won't you? I mean, the performance is coming fine, but the lines are . . ."

"Course I will, old boy, course I will. Scout's honour. Cross my heart."

"Oh, and I have got a note on—"

"Got to go." Michael Banks went across to get his coat and brief-case.

"Lines a problem?" Dottie whispered to Charles.

"Seem to be."

She nodded knowingly.

"He starts all right," said Charles, "but he can't keep it up."

"You can say that again."

And, once again, there was no doubt of the sexual overtone in Dottie Banks's words.

CHAPTER SIX

THE WEEKEND with chums in Chichester did not seem, on the Monday's showing, to have left Micky Banks much time to look at his lines. If anything, he was worse after the break; even the words he had remembered the week before were now coming out jumbled and confused.

"Don't worry," he kept saying. "Don't worry, Peter old boy. They will come. Just out of practice learning, you know. That's the trouble with doing all these films and tellies—you just have to remember a little bit for a short take. Forget what it's like learning a long part. But don't worry—be all right on the night. I once got up Iago in three days when I was in rep. If we just press on with the rehearsal, it'll come."

But it didn't. And indeed it was very difficult to press on with the rehearsal. In every production there comes an awkward jerky stage when the cast abandon their books for the first time, but for *The Hooded Owl* it seemed to be going on longer than usual.

And it had a knock-on effect. George Birkitt got lazy about learning his lines too. Charles remembered from working on *The Strutters* with him that George had always had an approximate approach to the text, relying, as did so many television actors, on a sort of paraphrase of the speeches which homed in on the right cue. Strong direction could make him more disciplined and accurate, but Peter Hickton was not well placed to bully George Birkitt. The latter could always turn round—and indeed did turn round—and say, "Sorry, love, I don't mind working on them, but there doesn't seem a lot of point in my giving up my free evenings when *the star* is unwilling to do the same."

He couldn't resist putting a sneer into the words. In spite of the success of *Fly-Buttons*, George Birkitt was not yet a star—and quite possibly never would be. He lacked the necessary effortless dominance of character. Deep down he was aware of this fact, and it hurt.

Charles hoped that George's assumption was right, that Michael Banks's difficulty in retaining the lines was just the product of laziness. If that were the case, then atavistic professional instincts and the terrifying imminence of the first night would ensure that he knew the part by the time they opened. But Charles had a nagging fear that it wasn't that, that Michael Banks really was trying, that he did go through the lines time after time in the evenings, but that his mind could no longer retain them. If that was the situation, it was very serious. And through the star's casual bonhomie at rehearsals, Charles thought he could detect a growing panic as the awful realisation dawned.

They were making so little progress on the Monday that Peter Hickton took the sensible decision and dismissed most of the cast at lunchtime; he would sit down with Michael Banks and George Birkitt all afternoon and just go through the lines. It was a ploy that often worked. Apart from the shame of being kept in like a naughty schoolboy, the constant automatic repetition of the lines taken out of the context of the play could often lodge them in the leakiest actor's mind.

And on the Tuesday morning it was seen to have had some effect. George Birkitt, whose main problem with the lines had been an unwillingness to look at them, showed a marked improvement. Michael Banks, too, started with renewed confidence and got further into the text than he ever had before without error. Relief settled on the rehearsal room. When he was flowing in the part, the company could feel his great presence and their confidence in the whole enterprise blossomed.

The first breakdown came about twenty minutes into the play. Needless to say, it was in a big speech. As ever, the start was confident. And, as ever, about three sentences in, Michael Banks faltered. The entire cast held their breath, as if watching a tightrope-walker stumble, and all let out a sigh of relief when he managed to right himself and make it through to the end of the speech.

But it was a symptom of things to come. In the next big speech, Michael Banks again stumbled. Again he extricated himself, but this time at some cost to the text. What he said was a vague approximation of what Malcolm Harris had written, and he didn't even give the right cue to George Birkitt, who spoke next.

This threw George, and he got his lines wrong. Being George, he didn't try to cover the fluff and press on; instead he said, "Sorry, love, but I can't be expected to get my lines right if I get the wrong feed, can I?"

The scene lurched forward again, but its momentum was gone. Michael Banks's eyes were lit with the panic of a man about to dry. And sure enough, he did. Peter Hickton tried another approach and threw one of his little tantrums. This didn't help at all. It just soured the atmosphere of the rehearsal, and left Michael Banks looking pained, like some huge animal, beaten for a transgression he does not understand.

For a show due to open for its first public preview in a week's time *The Hooded Owl* was in far from promising shape.

There was a run on the Tuesday afternoon for the producers. Paul Lexington and Bobby Anscombe sat through the whole play in silence.

It was excruciating. Consciousness of the audience made Michael Banks nervous, and nervousness scrambled the lines in his head even further. George Birkitt got through with only one prompt, but his performance was spoiled by the smug smile he wore throughout at the star's expense.

Eventually, half-way through the second act, as the play's climax approached, Michael Banks could stand it no longer. He snatched the prompt copy from the Stage Manager and read the rest of his part. The strength of the performance, as ever, increased, but it was worrying.

The play finished and there was silence. The actors drifted away from the centre of the room to the safety of the walls, where they picked up crosswords, fiddled with knitting, lit cigarettes and gave generally unconvincing impressions of people who weren't worried about what was about to happen.

Paul Lexington and Bobby Anscombe were sitting at a table in the middle of the room, engaged in a fiercely whispered conversation. The cast couldn't help hearing odd words. Bobby Anscombe seemed to be doing most of the talking. "Bloody terrible . . . amateur . . . when I put my money into something I don't expect . . . can't put that sort of thing into a professional theatre . . ." These fag-ends did not augur well for any public announcement that might be made.

And when it came, the announcement lived up to their worst fears. With a gesture of annoyance at something Paul Lexington had just said, Bobby Anscombe stood up and banged his hand down on the table.

"This is bloody awful. I've backed more shows than you lot have had hot dinners and I've never seen anything like this. Do you realise, a week on Thursday you're going to play this show to all the West End critics? At the moment none of them's going to sit through to the end. If I don't see a marked improvement by the end of the week, I am going to take my money out!"

Shock registered on every face in the room. Even Paul Lexington's boyish mask was shattered.

Bobby Anscombe had intended his ultimatum as an exit line, but he was stopped by Michael Banks, who had worked with him in the past and knew his volatile temper. He stepped forward, diplomatically. "Bobby, old boy, take your point. The show does look pretty shitty at the moment. Also take the blame myself. I just haven't got the hang of the lines yet. But don't worry. Give us a couple of days and you won't recognise it."

"I'd better not. There is nothing in it at the moment that I would want my name associated with."

"Now come on, Bobby. It's only me letting the side down," Michael Banks volunteered nobly. "I don't know my lines and I'm dragging down the rest of the cast."

"And why don't you know your lines?" Bobby Anscombe snapped. "Listen. You know how much money we're paying you. It's a bloody big investment. And when I invest that much, I reckon to get value for my money." He thumped the table with his fist. "I'm paying for a star actor who can do the job of acting, not some old has-been whose memory's gone."

It was as if every person in the room had been slapped in the face. They all flinched. Michael Banks's charm had worked on every one of them, and they hated this savage attack on him.

The star himself took it with dignity. "Fair comment. I agree, I should know the lines by now. And I will. Don't worry, once in rep. I learned all of Iago in three days."

"I'm not interested in what you've done in the past. My money is invested in what you can do now."

Once again, Bobby Anscombe intended this as a parting shot, but again he was stopped. This time the interruption came from an unexpected source, as Lesley-Jane Decker leapt to the defence of her idol.

"It's all very well you saying that, but do you realise that Micky only saw the script ten days ago? It's a huge amount to learn in that time."

Bobby Anscombe looked at her contemptuously. "I am not concerned about *actor's problems*. I don't give a toss how long he's had to learn the part or how difficult it's been. All I know is he's signed a contract to play the part properly, and at the moment he's not doing it. I am not getting my money's worth. I'm a business man with a reputation to think of. I've backed this show and I intend to make money out of it.

The only way that's going to happen is if it looks like a professional West End production. At the moment it looks like amateur night. The only way for it to look any different is for Michael to learn the bloody lines. Unless," he added with unpleasant irony, "anyone has any other ideas for picking it out of the shit . . . ?"

"You could revert to the original casting."

It was Alex Household who had spoken. He hadn't intended to. He looked as shocked as everyone else at his words. They had just come out. The build-up of frustration he had felt ever since he lost the part would not allow him to be silent. When given such a cue, the reply had to emerge.

The investor wheeled on him. "What, and put your name above the title? How many people do you think that'll bring in? At least, with Micky there, we can fill a few weeks of punters coming in to watch him dry. But who's going to come out to see a nonentity like you? I'll tell you—bloody no one!"

Alex may have had some response ready, but he got no chance to voice it, as Bobby Anscombe turned his fury on Paul Lexington.

"Not that anyone's going to come anyway at the moment. Where's the publicity? I haven't seen a single poster for this bloody show. I haven't heard anything on the radio, seen nothing in the press, nothing on the box. How are the punters meant to know there's a show on? Bloody E.S.P.?"

Paul Lexington looked subdued. "Publicity is being handled by Show-Off Enterprises."

"Never heard of them."

"They're part of Lanthorn Productions. Denis Thornton recommended them."

"Oh, did he? Well, you shouldn't trust him further than you can throw him. Are they doing the publicity for his new musical at the King's?"

"I think so."

"Oh well then, you won't see anything from them. The musical opens next week as well. They'll be putting all their efforts behind that."

"They've said they're going to do a big media blitz for us at the end of this week."

"Oh really? And you believed them? Good God, the management of this outfit's as bloody amateur as the acting!"

And with that exit line, Bobby Anscombe succeeded in making his exit.

Rehearsals on the Wednesday were somewhat desultory, because the person most in need of rehearsal was not there. Michael Banks was fulfilling his previous commitment to play Pro-Celebrity Golf for the BBC. This was intensely frustrating for everyone, because logic dictated that he wasn't going to get much opportunity to look at his lines between strokes. It was just a wasted day.

But Peter Hickton could not resist working. Back with his own cast, he was determined to keep them at it as long as possible, fulfilling his own need for manic activity. (Charles had developed a new theory about the director's passion for working so hard. As well as giving him moral ascendancy over the rest of the company, driving himself to exhaustion might also cloud critical judgement, so that comments would be made on the effort that had gone into the show rather than on its quality.)

Because of the star's absence, his understudy took on the role. Alex Household performed this function punctiliously, making no comment, but demonstrating a fluency with the lines which contrasted significantly with Michael Banks's constant breaks for prompts.

And yet, even though Alex gave a performance quite as good as any he had given in Taunton, he was not as good as Banks. The artifice showed. Charles was aware of it, all the rest of the cast were aware of it. And the petulant set of Alex Household's mouth showed that he was aware of it too.

Malcolm Harris, whose school had Games on Wednesday afternoons, had managed to get away to see the rehearsal. When Peter Hickton was finally persuaded to stop for the day, at about seven, Charles Paris walked with the author to the pub round the corner.

Malcolm Harris was aggrieved. "A complete waste of my time, coming to that rehearsal, with Michael Banks not even there."

"Didn't anyone tell you he wouldn't be?"

"No."

Oh dear. Another black mark against Paul Lexington, both as management and agent.

But not as black as the mark that the ensuing conversation was to put against the producer's name.

"I wouldn't mind," said Malcolm Harris, "but it does cost a lot, all this toing and froing up to London."

"I suppose Paul hasn't mentioned anything like expenses?"

"No chance."

No. Few producers would, unless pressed by their client's agent.

"I wouldn't mind, but I am pretty hard-up at the moment. Teachers aren't paid a fortune, as you know."

"No. Still, you must have had some royalties from Taunton."

"No."

"No?"

"I did ask Paul about that. He said he couldn't pay me."

"Couldn't pay you?"

"No."

Charles could just picture Paul Lexington saying it, his plausible face earnestly puckered as he explained the situation to his gullible client.

Malcolm Harris brightened. "No, but he offered me a very good deal."

"Oh yes?" Charles couldn't keep the cynicism out of his voice.

But the author did not appear to notice it. "He said that he couldn't pay me because he had to maintain his cash flow for the London opening, but what he would do was to let me regard what he owed me as a stake in the show." He grinned with triumph.

"So you become an investor?"

"Exactly. I'm now on a percentage, with the Taunton money as my stake. So, when the play starts making a lot, I get this extra money on top of my royalty!"

And if it doesn't make any money, thought Charles, you don't even get what's owing to you.

"And you accepted the deal just like that?"

"Oh yes, of course. I mean, it's a good deal. And, anyway, I didn't have any alternative."

"Did he offer you any alternative?"

"Yes, he said, if I insisted on having my Taunton money, he wouldn't be able to afford to bring the show in."

It was all horribly predictable. Once again Charles was astonished how easily Malcolm would fall for the oldest cons in the business. And once again, his estimate of Paul Lexington's integrity dropped a few notches.

"By the way," asked the author, "has Micky Banks learnt the lines yet?"

"Well . . ." replied Charles Paris evasively.

To his surprise, when they got to the pub, he found Valerie Cass sitting there over a large gin. She waved effusively and he couldn't pretend he hadn't seen her. "Charles darling, how lovely to see you."

66

"Yes, er . . . terrific. You know Malcolm, don't you?"

"Of course. We met in Taunton."

"Did we?"

"Yes. I'm Valerie Cass. Though you might not think it, I'm Lesley-Jane's mother."

"Why shouldn't I think it?' asked Malcolm Harris innocently. He was not skilled in the art of complimenting ladies.

Nor, as Charles had come to realise to his cost, was he skilled in buying rounds of drinks. Resigning himself, Charles asked, "Get you another one, Valerie?"

"Oh, just a teensy gin. Thank you, Charles."

"Malcolm?"

"Half of lager, please."

While he was getting the drinks, Alex Household came in to the pub, looking harassed. "Tomato juice, Alex?"

"Whisky, please."

"Make that another large Bell's, please. So you're hooked on the stimulants now, are you?"

"God knows I need something, Charles."

"Hmm. Look who's over there. The mother."

"Oh Lord. I can't face her."

"Come on."

Reluctantly, Alex followed Charles to the table and sat down. He and Valerie looked at each other as cordially as two people who loathe each other can.

"So where's my baby?" asked Lesley-Jane's mother.

"Don't know," said Charles. "She said she had to rush off after rehearsal."

Valerie looked piqued. "Oh, from what she said, I gathered she usually came round here."

"Quite often. Not tonight."

"You don't know where she is, Alex?" she asked sweetly. And then, with a touch of venom, "Or are you no longer the right person to ask?"

Alex spoke without emotion. "As far as I know, she has gone out to dinner."

"Oh, has she? Then we've both been stood up."

"So it would appear."

"Do you know who we've been stood up by?"

"The version I heard was that Lesley-Jane was going out to dinner with Michael Banks 'to go through his lines'."

"Oh," said Valerie Cass. And then, with a different intonation, "Oh." The news gave rise to mixed emotions in her. She was glad her daughter had stood up Alex Household. She was impressed that her daughter was out with someone of the eminence of Michael Banks. But at the same time, she was nettled that her daughter hadn't told her she was going out, and the sexual jealousy, which was so much part of their relationship, was irritated by the news. She responded by testing her own sexual magnetism on Charles. "Had you thought about eating?"

"Me? Eating? Oh, I'm not much of an eater. Had a pie at lunch. That does me for the day."

"Oh."

"Tell me, Alex," said Malcolm Harris suddenly, "how is Micky Banks doing on the lines?"

"Well . . ." Alex Household pursed his lips sarcastically. And, whereas Charles had left it at that, Michael Banks's understudy proceeded to tell the author just how much of a massacre the star was making of his play.

It was just the two of them left in the pub. Valerie Cass had left rather petulantly as soon as she had finished her gin, and Malcolm Harris, breathing imprecations against Michael Banks, had gone soon after (without of course, buying a round). Charles and Alex drank a lot, but Charles didn't feel the relaxation he normally experienced when getting quietly pissed with a fellow actor. Alex was too jumpy, too neurotic, too dangerous.

Towards the end of the evening, indiscreet with the unaccustomed alcohol, he suddenly said, "I don't think I can take it much longer."

"Take what?" asked Charles.

"The humiliation. The sheer bloody humiliation. You take a decision rationally. You say I'll do this or that, it'll be hell, but I know the stakes, I'll do it, I can cope. And then you do it, and it is hell, and you realise that you can't cope."

"You mean this understudy thing?"

Alex nodded unevenly. "That, and other things, yes. I just feel it can't go on much longer. There's got to be some resolution, something that breaks the tension."

"What sort of thing?"

"I don't know." Alex Household laughed suddenly. "Someone's death, maybe."

Thursday's rehearsals built up to a run in the afternoon. Whatever Michael Banks had done with Lesley-Jane the previous evening—and something in their manner towards each other suggested he had done something—it had not improved his grasp of the lines. In fact, he was worse than ever. It was as if his mind had a finite capacity for lines; put in more than it could hold and they would start to overflow. He would surprise everyone by getting a new speech right, but then show that it had been at the expense of other sections of dialogue. The fact could not be avoided: Michael Banks could no longer learn lines.

He was cold and hurt at the end of the run-through, knowing what was wrong and unable to admit it.

"Look, Micky," said Peter Hickton, "would it help if we were to go through the lines again this evening, just the two of us?"

"No, thank you," the star replied politely. "I'll go home and put them on tape. That sometimes helps."

"Are you sure there's nothing that—"

"Quite sure, thank you," came the firm reply. "Don't worry about it. I once learned all of Iago in three days when I was in rep."

But the old boast didn't convince anyone. Amidst subdued farewells, Michael Banks left the rehearsal room.

"Christ!" muttered Paul Lexington, momentarily losing his cool. "What the hell do we do now?"

"I haven't a clue," confessed Peter Hickton. "Just run out of ideas. Unless we start pasting bits of the script all over the set. God, if only it were television. There you can use autocue and idiot boards, but in the theatre there's no technology that can help you out."

"Oh," said Wallas Ward, the languid Company Manager. "I wouldn't say that."

CHAPTER SEVEN

THE FRIDAY'S rehearsals followed the pattern of the previous day. Followed it even down to the detail of Michael Banks not knowing his lines.

The strain was beginning to tell on him. The casual bonhomie was maintained with more difficulty. There was no arrogance in the man; he was desperately aware that he was letting down all his fellow-actors, and by one of the least forgivable of professional shortcomings. Knowing the lines was the basic equipment for the job. Actors throughout history had staggered on to stages in various states of alcoholic debility, but they had almost always got through the lines, or at least an approximation of them. Michael Banks knew how much he was showing himself up, but the lines just wouldn't come. The dark circles under his eyes suggested he might well have spent the entire night going through them on a tape recorder, but it hadn't helped. Every improvement was at the cost of another speech forgotten.

And he knew fully what was at stake too. He was aware of his responsibilities as a star. One of the reasons why people in his position were paid so much money was because their presence could often ensure the survival of a production and keep the rest of the company in employment. They were responsible for the complete show, which was why stories of stars giving notes to other actors or ordering changes in sets and costumes were not just examples of megalomania, but the desire to maintain the overall standard of whatever production they put their names to.

Michael Banks knew that *The Hooded Owl* was not up to the required standard. It was due to open in less than a week. It was due to be shown to the paying public in a preview on the Monday evening. More important than either of these, it was due to be run again on the Saturday afternoon in front of Bobby Anscombe. And if it didn't live up to the investor's rigorous standards, no one had any doubt that he would make good his threat of withdrawing his backing.

Consciousness of all these pressures did not improve Michael Banks's concentration and, together with fatigue, ensured that the lines were worse than ever on the Friday afternoon run.

The rehearsal ended in apathetic silence. The actors drifted uselessly to their belongings.

"Micky, could we have a quick word?" asked Paul Lexington, and the star, with the dignity of a man mounting the scaffold, went across to join the producer, director and Company Manager.

Conscious of the straining ears of the rest of the company, Paul Lexington led the little group out into the corridor. They were out for two or three minutes, during which no one in the hall spoke.

Michael Banks led them back in, saying, "No, I'm sorry, Paul. I couldn't think of it. I have a reputation to maintain."

"Do you have any alternative to suggest?" asked the producer, careless now of listening ears.

The star spread his hands in a gesture of frustration. "Only that somehow I'll get the lines. Somehow."

"Micky, you've said that for a fortnight, and there's no sign of it happening. We've got to do something."

"But not what you suggest. There must be some other way." And, to put an end to the conversation, he walked firmly off to pour himself a cup of coffee.

After a muttered colloquy with Peter Hickton and Wallas Ward, Paul Lexington announced, "O.K., everyone. We'll break there. Ten o'clock call in the morning. There's still a lot of work to do."

"You can say that again," murmured Alex Household, who was standing beside Charles, "but I fear it will all be in vain."

"Alex," said the producer, "could you just stay for a quick word?"

"Of course."

"I'm going round the pub," said Charles. "See you there maybe."

"Perhaps," Alex replied abstractedly. And looking at the glow of restrained excitement in the other actor's face, Charles knew that Alex Household thought he was about to get his part back.

It was nearly an hour before Alex appeared in the pub, and one look at his face told that his expectation had not been realised.

He no longer even mentioned his 'no stimulants' regime as he took the large Bell's from Charles.

"The nerve! The bloody nerve! I cannot believe it!"

71

Charles didn't bother to prompt. He knew it was all about to come out.

"Do you know what they have asked me to do? Cool as you like, Paul bloody Lexington has asked me to sit in the wings for the entire run of this play and feed Micky Banks his lines!"

"What, you mean to be a kind of private prompter, whispering at him right through the play?"

"No, it's a bit more sophisticated than that. This is a deaf-aid job."

"I'm sorry. I don't understand."

"Oh, haven't you heard of these things? It has been done before in similar circumstances. It's a new device, whereby, thanks to the wonders of electronics, a star can still give a performance without bothering to learn the lines."

"Explain."

"Very simple, really. It's a short-wave radio transmitter. Some lemon—me, if Paul Lexington has his way—sits in the wings feeding the part line by line into the transmitter. The character on stage, for reasons which may possibly be explained by the insertion of a line or two into the script, wears a deaf-aid . . ."

"Which acts as a receiver?"

"Exactly."

"But does it work?"

"It has worked in some very eminent cases. Has to be modern dress obviously, and ideally an elderly character. You can't have Romeo swarming up the balcony in doublet, hose and hearing aid. But the part Micky's playing . . . why not?"

"I'm amazed. I never heard of that being done."

"Well, now you know. And if ever you see an actor on stage with a deaf-aid that is not integral to the plot—be suspicious."

"Has Micky agreed to use it?"

"He's still blustering and saying he never will and he once learnt Iago in three days, but he'll have to come round. There's no alternative. Except for the obvious one."

"Which is?"

"Reverting to the original casting." Alex Household let out the words in a hiss of frustration.

"Which they won't now they've got Micky's name all over the posters."

"No, of course they won't."

"I agree, it's a bit of a cheek, asking you to do it."

"Oh, you should have heard the way it was put. Paul Lexington at his greasiest. Of course, Alex old man, it could be done by an A.S.M., but you do know the part so well, you could time it properly. And of course we would raise your money for doing it."

"By how much?" No actor could have resisted asking the question.

"Fifty quid a week."

"That's pretty good."

"Oh yes, Paul Lexington pays you well for totally humiliating yourself."

"So you told him to get stuffed, did you?"

"No, I haven't yet." A cold smile came to Alex Household's lips. "And do you know, I'm not sure that I will."

"You mean you'll accept it?"

"I just might."

"Good idea," said Charles soothingly. "Take the money and don't think about it. That's always been my philosophy."

"Yes." Alex's mind was elsewhere. "Because now I come to think about it, it could be a good job."

"Sure, sure."

"A position of power."

"Power?"

"Yes. How does one gain revenge for humiliation?"

"I've no idea." Charles didn't like the way the conversation was going. The old light of paranoia gleamed in Alex's eye.

"Why, you humiliate someone else."

"Maybe, but—"

"And if you're stuck in the wings feeding lines to some senile old fool who can't remember them . . ." he laughed harshly, " . . . then it's really up to you what lines you feed."

By the Saturday morning Michael Banks had accepted the inevitable. He sat in shamefaced silence while Paul Lexington explained to the company what was going to be done and was still silent, but attentive, while Wallas Ward, who had encountered the deaf-aid on a previous production, demonstrated the apparatus.

They started rehearsing with it straight away. Alex Household sat in a chair by the wall, smugly reading the lines into a small transmitter with an aerial, while Michael Banks moved about the stage area with the deaf-aid in his ear.

"We can't really work out sound levels properly until we get into the theatre. Better just work on timing the lines," advised Wallas Ward.

"Come the day," asked Alex languidly, "where will I perch? On the Prompt Side?"

"No. You'd be too near the Stage Manager's desk there, might pick up his cues on the transmitter. No, you should sit O.P." Wallas Ward used the theatrical jargon for the side opposite the Stage Manager.

"Fine," said Alex, obtrusively cooperative.

They started. It was not easy. Michael Banks was not used to acting with a voice murmuring continuously in his ear, and Alex Household found it difficult to time the lines right. If he went at the natural pace, Michael Banks got lost and confused, unable to speak one line while hearing the next. The only way they could get any semblance of acting was for Alex to speak a whole sentence, Michael to wait for the end, and then repeat it. This method didn't work too badly in exchanges of dialogue, but again it was disastrous in the long speeches. With all the waits as the lines came in, the pace slowed to nothing. The lines were coming out as written, but the play was dying a slow death.

Michael Banks struggled on gamely for about an hour, but then snatched out his ear-piece and said, "I'm sorry, loves. It's just not working, is it?"

"Persevere," said Wallas Ward. "Just persevere. It takes a long time to get used to it."

"How long? We don't have that much time."

"Keep trying."

It was painfully slow, but Michael Banks kept trying. His memory might have gone, but he showed plenty of guts.

Bobby Anscombe was due at three. Then they would do a run for him. By then they had to have mastered the device. By unspoken consent they worked on through their lunch-break. Every member of the company was willing their star to succeed.

Slowly, slowly, the pace started to pick up. Alex spoke more quickly and Michael Banks lost the flow less often.

It was a cooperative effort between the two. It had to be. Alex's task of dictating the pace was quite as difficult as Michael's of delivering the lines. And Charles noted with relief how Alex was rising to the challenge. Whatever resentments he might feel, whatever threats he might have voiced against the star, the understudy was now totally caught up in his task, spacing the lines with total concentration, caught up in the communal will for the subterfuge to work.

They staggered through the second act. It was half-past two, and the minutes were ticking away till Bobby Anscombe's appearance. The tension in the room built up, the concentration of the entire company focusing on Michael Banks, living every effort with him.

He was approaching the big speech about the Hooded Owl, the speech which Malcolm Harris had rightly claimed to be the centre of his play, the speech that the star had not once got through since he had abandoned his script. All was silent in the rehearsal room, except for the actors speaking their lines.

The big speech was the climax of a scene between Michael and Lesley-Jane, playing his daughter. The dialogue which ran up to it showed good pace, and the strength of the star's performance, absent in recent days, began again to show through.

The speech was partly addressed to the Hooded Owl of the title and ended with the bird in its glass case being smashed on the floor. Though this was to happen every night in the run, the Stage Management had requested that, to save on glass cases, the action should be mimed during rehearsal.

Lesley-Jane cued the big speech, and no one breathed. "But, Father," she said, "you will never be forgotten."

"Oh yes," said Michael Banks with new authority. "Oh yes, I will.

"Three generations of us have lived in this house. Three generations have passed through this room, slept here, argued here, made love here, even died here. And the only marks of their passage have been obliterated by the next generation. New wallpaper, new furniture, new window frames . . . the past is forgotten. Gone with no record. Unless you believe in some supernatural being, taking notes on our progress. A God, maybe—or, if you'd rather, a Hooded Owl . . .

"Why not? This stuffed bird has always been in the room. Imagine it had perception, a memory to retain our follies. Oh God, the weakness that these walls have witnessed! And this bird has lived through it all, has seen it all, impassively, in silence."

He picked up the glass case and looked at the bird reflectively. Then, with a sudden change of mood, he shouted, "Well, I'm not going to be spied on any longer!" and dashed it to the ground.

They all burst into applause. Lesley-Jane threw her arms round Michael Banks's neck. The sense of achievement was felt by every one of them. Not only had he mastered the lines, he had also delivered the speech with greater power than it had ever received, either by him in rehearsal, or by Alex in performance. And yet Alex had contributed. Something of his timing, something of his delivery had come into

75

Michael Banks's performance, giving it new depth and stature. The applause was for the joint effort.

It was five to three. Paul Lexington held up his hands for silence. His glowing face showed that he was aware of the breakthrough. "I think we're going to be all right. We'll stop it there. Thank you all for your hard work. Bobby'll be here in a minute, and I want you all to give him a performance that'll blast him out of his seat!"

The run was not perfect, but it was good. Occasionally the timing between Alex and Michael went and the star lost his lines, but for most of the play the flow was maintained. Bobby Anscombe, who had reacted badly when he had first heard of the deaf-aid idea, was forced to admit at the end that it might work. Like everyone else, he recognised that there was no alternative.

"O.K." he announced to everyone in his usual grudging style. "We're still in business. Just. But you're all going to have to work a darned sight harder. The last week's rehearsal has been a virtual write-off, and you're meant to be facing a preview audience on Monday."

"You think we go ahead with that?" asked Paul Lexington. Clearly cancelling the previews had been one option the producers had discussed.

"We'll go ahead. The show needs the run-in, and even if it's bad, there won't be too much word-of-mouth outside the business. And any word-of-mouth'd be better than what we've got at the moment. What the hell's happening on the publicity front?" He rounded on his co-producer as he asked the question.

"Show-Off say it's all in hand."

"A bit late to have it in hand. It should be out of hand and all over the bloody media by now. Is *anything* happening?"

"Micky's doing *Parkinson* tonight—the Beeb's sending a car about six, Micky . . ."

The star acknowledged this information with an exhausted nod.

". . . and then there's supposed to be an interview in Atticus in *The Sunday Times* tomorrow."

"Better than nothing, but where are the bloody posters?"

"Apparently some delay about those. You know, the people who put them up are quite difficult to organise."

"I know that . . ."

"But it's supposed to be sorted out now."

"I should bloody well hope so. We open on Thursday and at the

moment we've made about as much noise as a fart in a hurricane."
Bobby Anscombe turned to Peter Hickton. "All set for the get-in at the
Variety tonight?"

The director nodded with relish at the prospect of a sleepless night of
hard work.

"Tech. run tomorrow night and D.R. Monday afternoon?"

"That's it," Peter Hickton confirmed.

"Hmm. Well, for God's sake see that Micky and Alex get some
practice with that bloody walkie-talkie tomorrow afternoon. There's a
long way to go before it sounds natural."

"Don't worry," said Paul Lexington diplomatically. "We'll sort it out.
This is going to be a show you'll be proud to be associated with, Bobby."

The investor barked a short, cynical laugh. "Bloody well better be.
Don't forget, Paul, we still haven't got a contract. I can still pull out if I
don't like it."

"Yes, sorry about that. There's been so much on this week I just
haven't had time to get the details of the contract finalised."

Charles wondered whether this was true or whether Paul Lexington
was once again using delaying tactics for devious reasons of his own.
Distrust of the producer was now instinctive.

Bobby Anscombe gave an evil grin. "I don't mind having no contract
if you don't. Gives me the freedom to walk out at will."

But nobody believed his threat. They all knew that *The Hooded Owl*
had just survived a great crisis. For the first time that week, they all
dared to feel confident that the show would open the following
Thursday, as planned.

CHAPTER EIGHT

THERE'S NOTHING like a long Technical Run to dissipate any euphoria attached to a theatrical production, and that was the effect of the one held for *The Hooded Owl* on the evening of Sunday, 26th October, 1980.

As is often the case with such events, it started late. Peter Hickton had had trouble with the resident stage crew at the Variety over the Saturday night. He was used to working with crews who knew him and who, like his casts, were prepared to work round the clock to achieve the effects he desired. The staff of the Variety did not have this attitude. They had no personal loyalty to him and were too strongly unionised to accept his way of working. Peter Hickton, unaware that cooperation could be bought by payment of "negotiated extras", responded to the crew's apparent lethargy by throwing one of his tantrums, which had only served to make them less willing to help out. Paul Lexington and Wallas Ward had had to devote much energy to smoothing ruffled feathers, nobody had got much sleep, and everything was way behind schedule.

When eventually, after ten o'clock at night, the run started, it was very slow. Apart from the unfamiliarity of the entrances and exits and the other customary problems for the cast, Peter Hickton had not had time to complete the lighting plot, so much of that was being done in the course of the run, which meant endless waits while new lighting settings were agreed. This left the cast standing around; they got bored and giggly, which set off explosions of bad temper from the technical staffs working around them. The atmosphere degenerated.

Members of the resident stage crew wandered round, looking at their watches and making dark remarks about amateurism and provincial rep. and the folly of trying to bring in a show so quickly and the unlikelihood of its being presentable in time for the Monday night preview.

Paul Lexington rushed around, also looking at his watch and working out how much overtime he was going to have to pay (or, to Charles's suspicious mind, how much overtime he was going to avoid paying).

The latest technical innovation, the deaf-aid transmitter, did not make things any easier. For a start, the resident sound engineer didn't like it, because he hadn't been consulted about its introduction and he maintained that he should be responsible for all sound equipment. This led to a circuitous discussion with Paul Lexington about whether it was sound equipment or not, which was only settled after much wrangling (and, almost definitely, money changing hands).

But even when its use had been approved, it didn't work as it should. Michael Banks, who by this time looked terminally tired, seemed to have lost the knack of timing which he had so laboriously achieved the day before, and so his lines were once again all over the place. Alex, from his position in the wings, was not concentrating as much and could not easily be kept informed about when they were stopping and starting, going back to rehearse lighting changes and so on, with the result that he was often feeding the wrong words.

Setting the transmitter's volume level was also a problem. If it was too low, Michael kept mishearing lines and producing bizarre variations, many of which would, under other circumstances, have been funny, and did in fact produce some snorts of ill-advised laughter from the overwrought cast. If the level was set too high, Michael could hear all right, but unfortunately so could the rest of the theatre, in a sort of ghostly pre-echo.

But the climax of technical disaster came, as the climax always did, with the Hooded Owl speech. Charles was out in front and saw what happened.

It was then getting on for three in the morning, but in the last quarter of an hour things had been getting better. With the end of the play in sight, everyone seemed to get a second (or possibly tenth) wind. Michael Banks, for the first time in the run, showed some signs of his real power as the Hooded Owl speech drew near.

"But, Father," said Lesley-Jane, "you will never be forgotten."

"Oh yes. Oh yes, I will.

"Three generations of us have lived in this house. Three generations have passed through this room, slept here, argued here, made love here, even *picked up a passenger in Shaftesbury Avenue to take out to Neasden . . .*"

There was silence in the theatre. The star, suddenly aware of what he had said, looked pitifully puzzled. Charles wondered if Alex Household had carried out his threat of feeding the wrong lines. If so, he had chosen a singularly inappropriate moment for the experiment.

It was some time before the cause of the error was identified. The transmitter was on the same wave-length as a passing radio-cab.

79

Somehow the Technical Run ended. Somehow a Dress Rehearsal was achieved on the Monday afternoon. And somehow, not too long after eight o'clock on the Monday evening, the curtain rose for the first time on the London production of *The Hooded Owl* by Malcolm Harris.

It was just competent. To say more would have been to overstate the case, but as a first preview it got by. The West End had witnessed many worse first previews.

The house was about a third full and they were respectful if not ecstatic in their reaction. Those of the cast who remembered the euphoria of Taunton were disappointed, but they comforted themselves with the fact that they were at least *on*, something which three days previously had looked most unlikely.

Michael Banks managed his lines fairly well, with only a couple of mishearings and one awfully long thirty seconds where he totally lost the thread. Perversely, George Birkitt seemed to have lost his lines completely and had to take at least half a dozen prompts. Charles Paris was heard to remark cynically that George, having seen that the star had got a deaf-aid, thought he ought to have one too.

Though he got the lines, Michael Banks's performance was very subdued, only a vestige of what he could achieve. That was just the result of fatigue. The strains of the last fortnight were catching up with him, and he looked every one of his sixty-four years.

No one was too worried about it. After all, these were only previews. Wait till the first night they thought, and watch "Doctor Theatre" do his work.

Two more previews to go, and then, at seven o'clock on the Thursday (early so that the critics could get their copy in), the curtain would go up on the first night proper of *The Hooded Owl*.

"Hello, it's me."

"Charles."

"Sorry to ring you at school, but I wanted to get hold of you and I'm in the theatre in the evenings."

"Yes . . ."

"Can you talk, Frances?"

"Well, I've got someone with me, but if you're quick . . ."

"It's about the first night."

"Oh yes. Of your play. When is it?"

"Thursday."

"Ah."

"I wondered if you could come . . . ?"

"Thursday. Hmm. I am actually meant to be going to a meeting . . ."

"Frances . . ."

"But I suppose I could . . . Yes, all right, Charles. After all, I don't want to miss your opening in this wonderful part you told me about."

"Ah."

"What?"

"Hmm. It is a long time since we spoke, isn't it?"

"What do you mean?"

"I'm afraid you won't have the pleasure of seeing me onstage. Instead you will have the no doubt greater pleasure of sitting beside me."

"Why? What's happened?"

"I'll explain all on Thursday. See you in the foyer of the Variety Theatre in Macklin Street at quarter to seven."

"All right."

"Goodbye."

"Goodbye."

He shivered. Was it imagination, or did she really sound colder towards him?

There was a small reception after the Tuesday night preview. This was not Paul Lexington pushing the boat out for the cast, which would have been very out of character; it was for the ticket agencies.

Charles had forgotten how important these now were to the survival of a West End show. As transport costs rose and London's reputation for violence after dark grew, business was increasingly dependent on coachloads of theatre-goers coming in from the provinces. So the ticket agencies and the people who organised the coaches were very important and managements were wise to make a fuss of them.

Hence the reception, with bottles of wine and the odd crisp provided by Paul Lexington Productions. It was typical of the outfit that before the performance, the Company Manager, Wallas Ward, had come round the dressing rooms with a message from the management. The message had been that the reception was for the ticket agencies, and the cast were requested to ration themselves to one glass of wine each. It was like the old admonition at nursery teas, F.H.B. (Family Hold Back).

Charles thought it was appalling. He wouldn't have minded the meanness of only allowing one glass each, if it hadn't been that the reception was so timed as to prevent that vital half-hour in the pub before closing time, which was so much a part of the necessary wind-down from giving of himself in performance. (The fact that, as understudy, he wasn't giving a performance did not reduce the necessity for the wind-down.)

But the cast were all very professional and knew the importance of the agencies' backing, so they presented their most charming fronts. Needless to say, the focus of the visitors' attention was Michael Banks, who, in spite of his fatigue, made himself most affable and approachable. Charles admired the skill with which the old pro conveyed an air of ease and relaxation, of the company having been one happy family, of the great fun he had had rehearsing for the show. At one point he overheard the star laughing and saying, "Long time since I've done theatre. Even had a little trouble learning the old lines. Still, got that sorted out now."

As an exercise in the skills of understatement and of giving the wrong impression without actually lying, Charles thought that took some beating.

He himself got landed with a boring little man from Luton, who was a great stalwart of the local amateur dramatic society there and clearly, though he didn't quite put it into words, thought *The Hooded Owl* a pale shadow of their recent production of *When We Are Married*. "Also," he said expanding his criticism, "your show's too long."

"Oh really?" said Charles mildly. "You mean it sags?"

"No, but it finishes too late. Coach party'd be very late back to Luton, and they don't like that."

"Oh."

"What you want to do . . ." The man paused, then magnanimously decided to give the benefit of his expertise, "What you want to do is chop ten minutes out of it. Then you may have a show."

"Oh," said Charles. "Thank you very much."

It was Paul Lexington's party, and since courting the ticket agencies was very much a management job, Charles was surprised to notice that the producer wasn't there. Wallas Ward was filling in, exercising his rather effete charm on the guests, but it wasn't the same. Charles heard more than one question as to where Paul was. The ticket agents felt they weren't getting the full treatment.

The producer did finally arrive about half an hour into the party, and he scurried around meeting everyone, making up for his earlier absence. He did so with his customary boyish bounce, and yet there was something strange in his manner. His face had the dead whiteness of someone in shock. Charles wondered what new disaster had hit the production, or which of the producer's dubious deals had just blown up in his face.

He was soon to find out. The guests were eventually ushered out at about eleven forty-five. This took some doing, as they seemed prepared to stay all night. They didn't seem to share their clients' reservations about getting home late. It was only when the bottles of wine had been firmly put away and the last glass drained that they got the message. (Charles also got the message that he wasn't going to get the quick slurp of wine at the end of the evening that he had been promising himself.)

Etiquette had demanded that none of the cast should leave until the last of their guests had gone, but, as soon as the final raincoat disappeared round the door of the theatre bar, the entire company leapt for their belongings to make a quick getaway.

"Shall we go, Micky?" Charles heard Lesley-Jane Decker say to the star.

Which was in itself interesting.

But they were all stopped by Paul Lexington clapping his hands. "Listen, everyone. I have some news. I'm afraid once again it's good news and bad news. The good news is that we've got the ticket agencies on our side. They like the show and they're going to recommend it to their clients—on one condition.

"That condition is that we cut ten minutes out of the running time."

This was greeted by a ripple of protest. Malcolm Harris, who would have been the most vigorous protester, was not present, but Peter Hickton, acting on the author's behalf, remonstrated. "Look, we can't do that. The play's really tight now. We'll ruin it."

"Sorry," said Paul. "Got to be done. Anything'll cut down if it has to. Peter, see me in the production office at ten and we'll go through the script. Then we'll have a full cast call at two to give you the cuts. O.K., Wallas?"

The Company Manager nodded.

"We should let Malcolm know," protested Peter Hickton. "It is is his play."

"There isn't time. Anyway, it's not his play now. I've got the rights. I'm sorry it's necessary, but it is. We won't get the coach parties if the show ends as late as it does now."

If anyone needed evidence of the power of the ticket agencies, there it was. Grumbling slightly, but accepting the inevitable, the cast once again made to leave, but Paul Lexington again stopped them.

"Then there's the bad news."

They froze. They had all thought the cuts were the bad news.

"I've just come from a meeting with Bobby Anscombe. I am afraid we could not agree over certain . . . artistic matters. As a result, he has decided to withdraw his backing from the production."

This hit them like a communal heart-attack. As the shock receded, Charles found himself wondering what the disagreement had really been about. He felt certain that Paul Lexington had been trying to pull a fast one on his co-producer. Maybe the missing contract had finally appeared and Bobby Anscombe hadn't liked its provisions. It must have been something like that; Charles was beginning to understand the way Paul Lexington worked. But if he had tried to dupe the wily Bobby Anscombe as easily as the innocent Malcolm Harris, it was no wonder that he had come unstuck.

But, like the eternal Wobbly Man, the young producer bounced back. "Now this is a pity, but it's not a disaster. I would rather lose Bobby's backing than compromise my artistic integrity over this production."

The fact that no one laughed out loud at this remark suggested to Charles that they didn't all share his view of the man. For most of them, his plausible exterior was still convincing.

"There are other investors, and don't worry, I've still got plenty of backing for this show. I'm not going to go bankrupt. Don't worry about a thing. *The Hooded Owl* will go on, and, what's more, it'll be a huge success!"

But, in spite of the stirring words, in spite of the cast's cheers, Charles could see panic in Paul Lexington's eyes.

And when he thought about it, it didn't surprise him. He didn't know the details of the funding of the show, but he could piece a certain amount together. Paul Lexington Productions had been able to mount *The Hooded Owl* at Taunton, but had been unable to bring it into town without Bobby Anscombe's support.

And that support had been bought at the cost of considerably increasing the budget. With the Taunton cast, it remained a comparatively cheap show. But with Michael Banks's—and indeed George Birkitt's—names above the title, it was a much more expensive proposition.

And now the support, whose condition the cast changes had been, had been withdrawn.

Michael Banks was suddenly a very expensive albatross around Paul Lexington's neck.

CHAPTER NINE

THE UNDERSTUDY'S is a strange role, and never is he made more aware of its strangeness than on a first night. He is caught up in the communal excitement, without the prospect of release that performance gives. He cannot quite detach himself or even avoid nerves; he has to be eternally in readiness; only when the final curtain has fallen can he be sure he will not have to go on. During the "half" before the curtain rises, he has his twitchiest moments. He has to watch the actor he would replace for signs of strain or imminent collapse and wonder nervously whether he *could* actually remember the lines if he had to go on. Sometimes the worst happens, and the actor does not appear for the "half". Then the understudy goes through agonies of indecision before the Company Manager gives him the order to get into costume and make-up. And how often, as the understudy trembles in the wings awaiting the rise of the curtain, does the real actor appear, full of apologies about a power failure on the Underground or the traffic on the Westway.

It is almost impossible for the understudy to achieve mental equilibrium. His thoughts sway constantly between the desire to go on and the desire to settle down for a relaxed evening with a book in the secure knowledge that he won't have to go on. (This at least is true of *aspiring* understudies, those who really wish they had parts. There is a breed of professional understudy, often, if female, actresses who have semi-retired to bring up families, for whom the job is all that they require. It gives them the contact with the theatre that they crave, without the total commitment which acting every night demands.)

Charles Paris was not a professional understudy. He still had dreams. And, though those dreams had taken something of a battering since the heady days of Taunton, they were resilient and survived in amended

85

form. The image of suddenly being called in to take over from George Birkitt and astounding the critics with his unsung brilliance was one that would not go away, however hard he tried to suppress it.

He knew that that was one of the reasons why he went to see George Birkitt first on his back-stage round at the "half". The vulture instinct would make him acutely observant for any signs of imminent cerebral haemorrhage in the actor.

George Birkitt, however, looked remarkably fit. He was gazing into his make-up mirror, playing the same game that he always did on the monitor screens in television studios—in other words, deciding which was his best profile.

"Hello, George. Just dropped in to say all the best."

"Oh, thanks, Charles." He seemed completely to have forgotten that Charles had ever played the part. "I think the director and some of the cast of *Fly-Buttons* should be out front tonight."

He couldn't resist mentioning the television series, just in case anyone should forget he was in it.

"Oh great. I'll be out there."

"Good. Then you could do me a favour. You know in the dinner party scene, when I'm downstage doing my incest speech . . ?"

"Yes."

"Well, could you tell me what Micky's up to during that? I'm sure he makes some sort of reaction I can't see. Could you watch out for it? I mean, I know he's the star and all that, but I'm damned if I'm going to be upstaged, even by him . . ."

The Star Dressing Room was Charles's next port of call. Its door was guarded by Cerberus in the form of Micky Banks's dresser, Harve, a redoubtable old queen who had been with his master for years. Recognising the visitor, he said, "O.K., just a quick word. Don't want him tired."

"Fine."

In spite of his dresser's cares, Michael Banks did look absolutely shattered through his heavy make-up.

"All the best, Micky."

"Thanks, Charles old boy." The star smiled graciously.

"Sure you'll knock 'em dead tonight."

"Hope so, hope so."

There was a tap at the door and Harve grudgingly admitted Lesley-Jane Decker. As at Taunton, she was bearing gifts. The shape of the parcel she put on Michael's make-up table showed that, for him at least, she had graduated to full-size bottles of champagne.

She put her arms around his neck and said, "All you wish for yourself darling."

"Thank you, love. Same to you." Michael Banks grinned indulgently. "Is the redoubtable Valerie Cass up in your dressing room ready to give you lots of tips?"

Lesley-Jane laughed. "She's out front where she should be. With Daddy."

"She'll be round before the evening's out."

Charles felt awkward, excluded from their scene. "Well, I'll . . . er . . ." He edged towards the door, which Harve obligingly—indeed, pointedly—opened for him.

Outside stood Alex Household.

"Break a leg, Micky," he said with a rather strained intonation. "I'll be out there supporting you."

"Bless you." The star turned round to his understudy. "Couldn't do it without you, you know."

"I know." Alex Household gave the words perhaps too much emphasis.

Lesley-Jane could not keep her back to the door indefinitely and turned. Charles noted how pale she looked, almost ill.

"*Bonne chance*, Lesley-Jane," pronounced Alex formally. "See you're doing your rounds with the first night presents."

He said it deliberately to make her feel awkward. And succeeded.

"Yes . . . yes. I'm . . . er . . . afraid I didn't get round to doing anything for the understudies."

"No," Alex Household snorted with laughter. "No, of course not."

And, slamming the door, he left the Star Dressing Room.

Charles caught up with him in the Green Room. Alex's strange position in the production must have been making all of the usual understudy agonies even worse. Charles wanted to say something to help, but all he could think of was "Break a leg."

"Oh, you think you should wish luck to people who merely feed lines, do you? People whose job could be equally well—and probably better —done by a tape recorder."

"We all need luck," said Charles gently.

Alex laughed. "Yes, we do, don't we?"

Then he started trembling. His whole body shook uncontrollably. His teeth chattered and he whimpered.

"Are you all right?"

"Yes, I'm . . . Yes, I'm . . . Yes, I will be."

And, sure enough, he soon had control of himself again. The shivering subsided.

"Sure you're O.K.? There'll be St. John Ambulance people out front."

"No, I'm all right." But Alex's eyes belied his words. They were wide with fear. "This is how it started last time."

"How what started?"

"The breakdown." And he was seized by another spasm. The worst of it passed, but his teeth still chattered feebly.

"Are you cold or . . ?"

"Cold? No. Or if I am now, I won't be later. I'll be roasting. Have you any idea how hot it gets in my little solitary nest on the O.P. side? Don't worry, I'll be hot enough. In fact, I'll take this off while I think."

He hung his jacket on a hook in the Green Room. As it swung against the wall, there was a thud of something hard in the pocket.

Alex Household gave a twisted smile and announced ironically, "Right, here we go. Tonight will be the climax of my career. Twenty-three years in the business has all been the build-up for this, as I take on my most challenging role ever—bloody prompter!"

"Come on, Alex. It's not so bad, it's—"

"Isn't it? What do you know about how bad it is?"

Charles retreated under this assault. "I just meant . . . Never mind. Back to what I said first—break a leg."

"I should think that will be the very least I will break," said Alex Household, and walked towards the stage.

Charles knew it would be unprofessional to use the pass-door from backstage to the auditorium once the house had started to fill, so he went out of the Stage Door to walk round.

The first thing he came across outside was Malcom Harris being sick in the gutter.

"Are you O.K.?"

"Yes, I . . . will be."

"Don't worry. It's going fine. And at least Micky's deaf-aid thing guarantees that he does actually say the lines you wrote."

88

"Yes, I suppose so." The schoolmaster looked up at him pitifully. "I just don't think I can sit out there and watch it all. I'm so jumpy, I'll be sick again or . . ."

"Then don't sit there. Stand at the back, go backstage, go out for a walk, do whatever makes you feel most relaxed."

"But if I don't sit in my seat, I'll be leaving my wife and my wife's mother on their own."

"Well, you could do that, couldn't you?"

"Yes, I suppose I *could*." But obviously it was an idea that had never occurred to him before, and his mind would take a little while to accommodate it.

"Frances, I'm sorry I'm late."

"When were you ever otherwise?"

"I wasn't late for that meal in Hampstead." Even as he said it, he wished he hadn't. There was something about the memory of that evening that made him uneasy. He kissed her clumsily to change the subject.

"Anyway, what is all this? Why aren't you going to be onstage? When we last met, you told me . . ."

"I'll explain. Have we got time for a drink?"

They would have had, but there was such a crush in the bar, there was no prospect of getting served before the curtain went up. Which was annoying.

While they reconnoitred the bar and found their seats (on the aisle, so that, if his services as an understudy were required, Charles could be quickly extracted), he gave Frances a brief résumé of how he had lost his part.

"Well, I think that's rotten," she said, with genuine annoyance.

It cheered Charles, to hear her angry on his behalf. He took her hand and felt the scar on her thumb, legacy of an accident with a kitchen knife in the early days of their marriage. Accumulated emotion made him weak, needing her.

"Charles!"

"Well, if it isn't that naughty Charles Paris . . ."

"With his lovely wife . . ."

"Frances, isn't it? Oh, it's been so long . . ."

"An absolute age . . ."

This stereo assault on them came from two men in late middle age, bizarrely costumed in matching Victorian evening dress. Instantly

Charles recognised William Bartlemas and Kevin O'Rourke, a pair of indefatigable first-nighters.

"And how *are* you, Charles?" demanded Bartlemas.

"Yes, how *are* you?" echoed O'Rourke.

Neither waited for a reply as they galloped on. "Are you still up to your naughty detective things we hear so much about?"

"Yes, *are* you?"

"No, not at the moment. I—" was all he managed to get out.

"Another first night. I don't know . . ."

"Not as glittering as it should be, is it, Bartlemas. . . ?"

"No, not really *glittering*, no . . ."

"So few people dress up for first nights these days . . ."

"It is disgraceful . . ."

"Appalling . . ."

"That lot . . ." he gestured to a large block of seats full of people in evening dress, "have made the effort . . ."

"Yes, but they're Micky Banks's chums . . ."

"Oh well . . ."

"At least that generation knows how to behave at a first night . . ."

"*That* generation, dear? They're *our* generation!"

This witticism reduced both of them to helpless laughter. But not for long enough for Charles or Frances to say anything.

"Lot of paper in tonight, isn't there?" said Bartlemas, looking up to the Circle and Gallery.

"Lot of paper, yes . . ."

"Paper?" Frances managed to query.

"Free seats, love. Often happens for a first night if it's not selling . . ."

"Yes, blocks of tickets sent round the nurses' homes, that sort of thing . . ."

"Believe me, love, if you go to as many first nights as we do, you get to recognise them . . ."

"Recognise individual nurses even . . ."

"There's one with a wall-eye and a wart on her nose who I swear goes to more first nights than we do . . ."

This also was apparently a joke. They roared with laughter.

"Why is there so much paper?" Charles managed to ask.

"No publicity, dear . . ."

"And the theatre's out of the way . . ."

"People'd flood to see Micky Banks . . ."

"Simply flood . . ."

"But they've got to know where he is . . ."

"As you say, no publicity . . ."

"*By* the way, who's Dottie with tonight?"

"Don't know, but looks such a nice young man . . ."

"Joy-boy?"

"Maybe . . ."

"Oh," said Charles. "You mean she and Micky don't . . ."

"Now you don't want us telling tales out of school, do you?"

"Oh, you naughty Charles Paris, you . . ."

They seemed set to continue talking forever, but the auditorium lights began to dim, so they scuttered off, giggling, to find their seats.

Charles and Frances sat down too. And with feelings too complex to itemise, he watched the curtain rise on the first official London performance of *The Hooded Owl*.

The applause at the interval was very generous. It almost always is on a first night, when the audience tends to be Mums, Dads, husbands, wives, lovers and friends-in-the-business. But, even allowing for that, Charles reckoned they were enjoying it.

Michael Banks was giving a performance of effortless authority. Some of the *cognoscenti* had recognised why he was wearing the deaf-aid, but for the majority, it just seemed to be part of the character, justified by a couple of new lines.

The performances were all up, with the possible exception of Lesley-Jane Decker, who seemed to be giving a little less than usual. Probably the result of nerves at her first West End opening.

But what also shone through was how good a play *The Hooded Owl* was. It was very conventional, even old-fashioned, but its tensions built up in just the right way, and it gripped like a strangler's hand.

Charles looked round to where he knew Malcolm Harris should be, but the seat between the ferret-faced women was empty. The author had taken his advice and was presumably prowling around somewhere. His ferret-faced women looked unamused by his absence.

Charles and Frances joined the exodus to the bar and met another couple coming towards them. The man was unfamiliar, but there was no mistaking the woman with her subsidised red hair.

"Charles, darling!"

"Oh. Valerie. I don't think you know my wife, Frances . . ."

"But of course I do. We met in Cheltenham."

"Did we?" asked Frances, clueless as to whom she was addressing.

"Yes, yes, all those years ago."

"Oh."

"And this . . ." said Valerie Cass, with no attempt to disguise her contempt, "is my husband."

He was twenty years older than his wife, and looked meek and long-suffering. As indeed he would have to be. Either that or divorced. Or dead.

"Oh God," Valerie Cass cooed. "I know what you must be feeling, Charles. I feel it myself. Just aching to be up there with them. Only we who have worked in the theatre can understand the ache."

She raised one hand dramatically to her forehead. She was wearing long evening gloves, indeed seemed to be fully dressed for a ball.

"Oh, it's not so bad," Charles offered feebly.

"And I'm so worried about Lesley-Jane," she emoted.

"Why?"

"The performance just isn't there."

"Oh, I wouldn't say that. She's a bit subdued, but she's—"

"No, it's more than that. I know that girl, know her as only a mother can, and I know she's not well. I think I'd better go backstage and see what's the matter."

"Oh, I don't think you should," her husband interposed mildly. "Wait till the end. I'm sure you shouldn't go round in the middle of a performance. Not the thing at all."

"And what . . ." she withered him with a glance, "what do you know about it?"

And she stalked off to the foyer.

Mr. Decker grinned weakly, made a vague gesture with his hand and moved off down the aisle to buy an ice-cream.

The crush in the bar was worse than before the show, but this time Charles was luckier. Lucky to the extent of meeting a friend who had had the foresight to order a bottle of champagne for the interval.

"Gerald!"

The solicitor looked immaculate as ever, in perfectly-tailored evening dress. His wife Kate also looked perfect. She and Frances fell on each other. They hadn't met for years. Used to be great friends, before Charles walked out. Used to go around as a foursome. Guilt was added to the turmoil of Charles's feelings.

Gerald fought to the bar for a couple more glasses and generously shared the bottle.

"Doing any detective work, Charles?" He had helped the actor on one or two cases and found an enthusiasm for investigation which he could never muster for his extremely lucrative solicitor's practice.

"No," Charles replied with satisfaction. It was pleasant not to have the complexities of crime on his mind for a change.

"Pity."

"But why are you here, Gerald? Got money in it?"

Gerald was quite a frequent "angel", though he kept his investments very secret, and winced at Charles's question. "No, in a sense I'm here under false pretences. I was coming because a client was involved as a backer, but he's no longer involved and . . ."

"Bobby Anscombe?"

"Right."

"Yes. I gather he had an 'artistic disagreement' with Paul Lexington."

"'Artistic disagreement'—my foot! You should have seen the contract Lexington tried to get him to sign."

Charles was glad to have his surmise confirmed. "Yes, I shouldn't think anyone steals a march on Bobby Anscombe."

"Or me, Charles. Or me."

Just as he was returning to his seat, Charles met Malcolm Harris rushing up the aisle. The author had reported in to his ferret-faced women, but was now off again.

"I should think you're pleased, aren't you?" asked Charles genially.

"Pleased?" hissed the schoolmaster. "That bastard Banks is just making nonsense of it."

"What do you mean?"

"I mean he's cutting great chunks. Big speeches—just because he doesn't like them, just cutting them out."

"But, Malcolm, *he*'s not making the cuts. They were made yesterday for—"

But the author was already out of earshot.

Oh dear. Another black mark for Paul Lexington's liaison and diplomacy.

The audience settled quickly after the interval and was soon once more caught up in the mounting dramatic tension of *The Hooded Owl*. Charles found himself swept along too. He realised that the cuts forced on the production had in fact helped it. By trimming down the first act, they kept the pace going, and the second act benefited.

93

And Michael Banks was growing in stature by the minute. Once again, Charles was aware of Alex Household's contribution to the performance. With him timing the lines, the star could concentrate just on the emotional truth of his acting, and the result was very powerful.

The Hooded Owl speech approached, and Charles felt the excitement building inside him. As ever, it would be the climax; this time the climax of one of the finest performances he had ever witnessed.

The scene of father and daughter in the bedroom began. Lesley-Jane was still low-key, but it did not seem to matter. It almost helped. The pallor of her acting threw into relief the power of Michael's.

"But, Father," she said, "you will never be forgotten."

"Oh yes. Oh yes, I will."

They stood facing each other. Maybe, over her shoulder, he could see his faithful feed in the wings. Probably not. He was too deeply into the part to see anything outside the stage.

The silence was so total that the auditorium might have been empty.

"Three generations of us have lived in this house. Three generations have passed through this room, slept here, argued here, made love here, even died here. And the only marks of their passage have been obliterated by the next generation. New wallpaper, new furniture, new window frames . . . the past is forgotten. Gone with no record. Unless you believe in some supernatural being, taking notes of our progress. A God, maybe—or, if you'd rather, a Hooded Owl . . ."

As he mentioned the bird, he turned his back on Lesley-Jane to look at it in the glass case. Every eye in the audience followed him.

"Why not? This stuffed bird has always been in the room. Imagine it had perception, a memory to retain our follies. Oh Lord!—"

Something had gone wrong. The audience did not know yet, but Charles, so familiar with the script, knew.

Slowly Michael Banks wheeled round. He looked puzzled, and seemed to be looking beyond Lesley-Jane into the wings.

"No," he said. "No, put it down. You mustn't do that to me. You daren't. Please. Please, I—"

There was a gunshot. Michael Banks clutched at his chest and slowly tottered to his knees. Lesley-Jane turned to look into the wings, and screamed.

The tableau was held for a moment, and the curtain swiftly fell.

The audience didn't know. Still they weren't sure. Was this a bizarre new twist of the plot? What had happened? The darkened auditorium was filled with muttering.

Then the houselights came up. The curtain twitched and the Company Manager, Wallas Ward, resplendent in midnight blue dinner jacket, appeared through the centre.

"Ladies and gentlemen, I regret to have to inform you that, due to an accident to Mr. Banks, we will be unable to continue the performance."

He did not say that the accident which had befallen Mr. Banks was death by shooting.

And he did not say that, even if they'd wished to finish the play with his understudy, they couldn't, because Alex Household had run out of the theatre immediately after the shooting.

CHAPTER TEN

CHARLES GOT round to the Stage Door as quickly as he could. Frances followed silently. One of her good qualities was the ability to keep quiet when there was nothing appropriate to say.

They were there before the rush. There were a few people milling around, but not yet the main surge of puzzled well-wishers, police, press and sensation-seekers.

Charles found the Stage Doorman, who was already regaling a little circle of cast with what he had seen. The murder had only occurred ten minutes before, but the old man already saw himself in the role of vital witness, and was polishing the phrases in a story which he would tell many times.

"I heard the shot over the loudspeaker. I knew there was something wrong. I've heard that play so many times in the past few days, I knew the lines wasn't right. Mind you, then I didn't know it was a shot. Could've been something falling over onstage, or a light-bulb blowing . . . but something inside me knew it was serious. I felt like a cold hand on my heart . . ." he paused dramatically, relishing the metaphor; which he then spoiled by mixing it, " . . . as if someone had walked over my grave.

"Next thing I knew Mr. Household was rushing past me out of the door. It was so quick. I didn't have time to stop him," he said, suggesting that under any other circumstances he would have downed the suspect with a flying tackle. "Not, of course, that I realised what he'd done then. I didn't know he'd just shot Mr. Banks."

"Are you sure he had?" asked Charles.

"Well, of course he had."

"I mean, was the gun in his hand?"

"No," the old man was forced to concede, "but—"

"Was he wearing a jacket?"

"I think so. I didn't notice. It was very quick, like I said." The old man sounded testy. Charles's questions were spoiling his narrative flow.

"Wait here a minute, Frances." He went through to the Green Room, hoping that he'd find Alex's jacket still hanging there, with the gun still cold in its pocket, with all five shots still unfired.

Alex was a prickly person, an unbalanced person, sometimes an infuriating person, but Charles didn't want to think of him as a murderer.

Various members of the cast were lolling about the Green Room, in various stages of shell-shock. George Birkitt was looking distinctly peeved, aware that Michael Banks had upstaged him in a way that was quite unanswerable. In a corner Malcolm Harris slumped on a chair, pale and whimpering.

The coat-hook was empty. Exonerating Alex wasn't going to be that easy. And was exonerating him appropriate anyway? All the evidence so far pointed to the fact that he had done the killing.

Charles wandered through the door on to the stage, and found even more evidence. Clinching evidence.

Backstage the overhead working light gleamed on something metal that lay discarded by the door. Charles recognised it instantly.

It was the Smith and Wesson Chiefs Special revolver that he had first seen in the Number One dressing room of the Prince's Theatre, Taunton.

He knelt down and, so as to avoid leaving fingerprints, felt the barrel with the back of his hand.

It was warm.

Depression flooded through him like fatigue. He didn't quite know why he'd hoped that Alex could be cleared of the murder, but the confirmation of his friend's guilt sapped him of all energy.

He left the gun where it was. The police would find it soon enough.

Back at the Stage Door, Frances looked at him and, instantly reading his emotional state, took his hand.

"Shall we go?"

"I don't know. I feel I should stay around, try and find out what's happened and . . ."

But the decision was made for him. The police had arrived while he had been on stage, and a uniformed constable was now clearing the growing crowd round the Stage Door.

"All right, if you could move along, please. There's nothing to see, and we've got a lot to do, so we'd be very grateful if you could just go home. Come on, move along, please."

He came face to face with Charles and Frances. "On your way, please.

On your way. Unless you're connected with the show, could you go home, please."

"I'm a member of the cast," said Charles.

"Oh. Were you backstage during the show?"

"No, actually I was in the auditorium."

"Well, in that case, could you go home, please. You'll hear anything there is to hear in the morning."

Not only excluded from performing, the understudy was not even to be allowed to take part in the murder investigation.

"Come along," said Frances. "Come home with me."

Back at the house in Muswell Hill, they went upstairs and stood on the landing. "I think the spare room, Charles," she said.

He nodded. She hadn't said it unkindly, and, in the state he was in, it seemed appropriate. And, in spite of it, he felt closer to her than he had for months.

The tensions of the week had taken their toll and he slept instantly. He had no dreams. But when he woke at quarter past six, his mind was full of ugly images, of Alex trembling, of the gun, and, most of all, of the expression of bewilderment and betrayal on Michael Banks's face as he clutched at his chest and sank to the ground.

To frighten off these visions, and because further sleep was out of the question, he went downstairs to make some tea. It was strange being in the kitchen of the house they had shared. He was aware of the parts of it that remained unchanged and equally of the innovations. Nothing could he view without emotion. He saw Frances had bought a dishwasher. Yes, time was precious. She was a busy lady these days.

And she wanted to sell the house. That thought disturbed him almost more than the events of the previous night.

The kettle boiled. He warmed the pot, instinctively found the tea in the caddy Frances's Auntie Pamela had given them as a wedding present, and brewed up. He arranged two mugs and a milk-bottle on a tray with the pot, and took them upstairs.

The door was ajar, and he pushed it gently open. Frances was still asleep. She lay firmly in the middle of their double bed, as he supposed she must do every night. In repose her face looked relaxed, but the fine network of wrinkles round the eyes showed her age.

He felt great warmth for her. Not desire at that moment, just warmth. He must never lose touch with her.

He put the tray down on the dressing table, and the noise woke her.

She started, unaccustomed to anyone else in the house, but when she saw him, she smiled blearily.

"Charles. Good gracious. A cup of tea in bed. I can't think when you last did that for me."

"When you were pregnant with Juliet, maybe."

"Probably."

He poured the tea. He felt slightly awkward, as though he were in a strange woman's room. He passed a mug to her and she propped herself up on the pillows to accept it.

"You feeling better this morning, Charles?"

"Yes, thank you."

"You looked terrible last night."

"Yes, I felt it. Thank you for salvaging me."

"Any time."

They were silent. There was still a restraint between them.

Frances moved over positively to switch on the radio. "See what's happening in the world," she said breezily.

"Hmm." Radio Four murmured earnestly from the speaker. "Are you still thinking of selling the house?" Charles blurted out.

"Yes. It's with the agents."

"Oh."

"Mind you, they say the market's pretty slack at the moment. And the trouble is I'm only here in the evenings to show people around. So I think it may take some time."

"Yes." This information made Charles feel disproportionately cheerful, as though he had suddenly been reprieved from something.

He became aware that the radio was talking about Michael Banks. Someone was giving an appreciation of his career. They must have worked fast to get it together, Charles thought. A busy night for them.

And no doubt a busy night of police questioning for *The Hooded Owl* company at the Variety Theatre. A lot must have been happening while he had slept.

The appreciation of Michael Banks was made up of interviews with his friends in the business. It was remarkable how many eminent names had allowed themselves to be woken up in the middle of the night to talk about him. And remarkable with what unanimity of love they spoke.

But, as Charles knew, Michael Banks had been a person who inspired love. For the first time since the shooting, Charles felt, not shock, but a sense of the tragic waste of his death.

For Alex he felt nothing but pity. The killing had not been a rational act; when he did it, Alex Household had been mentally ill. Charles felt guilty for not having recognised the seriousness of the actor's state. Maybe he could have done something to avert the tragedy . . .

"*But what of the show?*" asked the radio presenter. "*Needless to say, no reviews of* The Hooded Owl *have appeared in the papers today, but from all accounts the play was being very well received when the tragedy occurred. But surely Michael Banks's death must end the run before it had even started. Apparently not, according to the show's producer, Paul Lexington.*"

Paul's familiar voice came on, tired but as confident as ever. "*No. Of course, we are all shattered by what has occurred, but we are professionals. It is our job to entertain the public and that is what we will continue to do. Don't worry, the show will go on.*"

"*How soon?*"

"*Tonight. There will be a performance of* The Hooded Owl *tonight.*"

"*Tonight? But can you replace Michael Banks at that sort of notice?*"

"*Yes, we can.*"

"*But I understood . . .*" The interviewer picked his way carefully around the *sub judice* laws. "*I understood that Mr. Banks's understudy is . . . not available.*"

"*That is true. The part will be taken by another member of the company.*"

"*May I ask his name?*"

"*Certainly. His name is Charles Paris.*"

"*Who?*" asked the interviewer.

"WHO?" echoed Charles Paris.

CHAPTER ELEVEN

THE NERVES on the first night at Taunton had been bad; so had the understudy nerves of the first night at the Variety; but they were nothing to the sheer blind terror that attended Charles Paris as he waited to go on stage in the role in which Michael Banks's career had been so tragically cut short the night before.

Charles had not really believed it would happen. After hearing his name on the radio, he had thought it must be just bravado on Paul Lexington's part, the young producer falling into cliché, insisting that the show must go on when all logic showed it was impossible. He must have been interviewed during the night of panic following the murder; in the rational light of dawn he would recognise that his words had been just heroics.

Charles had so convinced himself of this that he didn't ring in to the production office until ten-thirty, deliberately giving the producer time to sober up his intoxicated imagination.

"Charles!" said Paul Lexington's voice. "Where the hell have you been? I've been ringing your number for hours."

"Ah. Well, I didn't actually spend the night at home."

"Well, now you have rung, get in here as quickly as you can. Where are you?"

"Muswell Hill."

"Get a cab and charge it."

"But what's the hurry?" asked Charles, deliberately obtuse.

"You're going on tonight playing the father."

Charles took a deep breath, mustering the arguments he had prepared. "Paul, I don't know if you have realised this yet, but I am not the understudy to the part of the father. I am understudying George Birkitt, who, when I last saw him, was looking as fit as a flea."

"Charles, this is an emergency! It's not the time to argue about the small print of your contract. I'll sort out the extra money with your agent."

101

"That is not what I'm arguing about. If I could play the part of the father for you tonight, I would be happy to oblige. But the point you seem to have missed is that I don't know the lines."

"Nor did Michael Banks."

"No, but . . . Good Lord, you don't mean . . . ?"

But that was exactly what Paul Lexington *did* mean. If Michael Banks could get through the part having his lines relayed to him by radio, then so, the producer's reasoning ran, could any other actor. And since Charles knew the production so well, he'd be able to remember the moves and . . .

Anyway, the show had to go on that night. Paul had given public undertakings on national radio and television that it would. His boast would also be in the later editions of the evening papers. It was a God-given publicity opportunity.

Charles was prepared to contest the definition of "God-given" under the circumstances, but Paul didn't give him time. "Find that cab and be here ten minutes ago!" he ordered before putting the phone down.

It was a strange day, most of which Charles walked through in a dream. What remained of the morning was to be spent acclimatising himself to the deaf-aid receiver and learning how to pace himself with the A.S.M. who was going to feed the lines.

That was agony. Charles kept remembering what Micky Banks had gone through at the same stage, and often, like his predecessor, was ready to throw in the towel and say it was impossible. His mind wasn't up to speaking one line while listening to another, and at the same time trying to remember the next move. His familiarity with his own original part didn't help either. In the scenes where the father talked to the character now played by George Birkitt, he kept hearing the father's line in his ear, mistaking it for his cue, and coming in with George's line. There seemed no prospect of his ever getting the technique.

He bashed away at it with the A.S.M. solidly from eleven-fifteen, when he arrived at the theatre, until half past two, without any break for lunch or the drink he desperately craved. The rest of the cast were called for three to do a complete rehearsal of all the scenes he was in.

And, suddenly, just as had happened to Michael Banks, at the eleventh hour the rhythm started to come. Partly it was familiarity with the lines after three hours of going through them, but also it was a kind of relaxation that came with the acceptance of disaster. This is never going to work, Charles was thinking, so what is the point of worrying about it?

With that thought came relief, and with relief sufficient detachment for him to split his mind, to let one part concentrate on hearing the lines, and the other on performing. The only sensation he could equate it with was that remoteness that comes during a long run, when the lines of the play get delivered every night, but the actor's mind is miles away, thinking about anything but the performance he is giving.

The rest of the company was wonderfully supportive. They all looked shattered after the shock and lack of sleep of the night before, but they all worked for him, recognising his need as only professional actors can. The only one who was less than whole-hearted in his support was George Birkitt, whose mind seemed to be on something else (no doubt whether his billing would be affected by Michael Banks's demise, and whether it was really appropriate for him to stay in the show and play a smaller part than Charles Paris).

But all the others demonstrated the unshakable freemasonry of actors in a crisis. They were all very sharp and attentive, prepared to go back over scenes or lines as often as was required, patient when Charles lost the line, encouraging when he got a flow of dialogue working.

Through his haze, Charles realised that it wasn't just the crisis that made them so deferential; it was the part he was now playing, too. Willy-nilly, he was now the star of *The Hooded Owl*, and the rest of the cast were giving him a taste of the treatment afforded to stars. It was something Charles Paris had never before experienced, and it felt very strange.

And so, like a grotesque dream, the hours passed. The "half" came. Charles made himself up for the new role, and dressed in the new costume. Fortunately, the latter was really new. Apart from the fact that Michael Banks had been bigger than he was, the dead man's clothes were still being examined by the police. Which was a relief to his replacement.

As he was preparing, all the company came in with good wishes and pledges of support. Paul Lexington exhorted him to do his best. The house was full, he said. As he thought, all the publicity had paid off.

The young producer looked buoyant. Charles wasn't too distracted to have the thought that Michael Banks's replacement must have considerably reduced the running costs of the production.

Then came the reassuringly calm voice of the Stage Manager over the loudspeaker. "Beginners, Act One, please. All the best, everyone."

Charles rose from his seat and walked out of the dressing room. As he closed the door, he noticed for the first time that there was a star on it.

103

The dream continued during the performance, but its nightmare quality receded. Once the sheer terror subsided and Charles realised both that he wasn't going to pass out and that he could manage the lines, he even began to enjoy it. He had forgotten the pleasure of playing a major part in a good play in the West End. (Well, to be honest with himself, he had to admit that "forgotten" wasn't the right word. But he did enjoy the unfamiliar experience.)

The performance was not without mishap. He did lose the lines on more than one occasion and threshed around helplessly through pauses that seemed eternal, until the A.S.M.'s quiet voice in his ear managed to get him back on to the right track. But these moments did not seem to lose the play's tension. The concentration of the cast was so strong that the mood was well maintained.

The audience kept up their concentration too. They all knew what had happened the previous night and, from Wallas Ward's announcement before the curtain rose, they knew that Charles had stepped in at very short notice. They didn't know about the device of the hearing-aid, but that was a point in Charles's favour; it made his feat of getting through the part even more remarkable. As he stood on the stage he felt pouring out from the audience that most British of reflexes: the will for the underdog to win.

He spent the interval just sitting in his dressing room, gathering his strength for the next act. People came in and out, but he didn't really notice them or their words of encouragement.

In the second act, he felt the power of Malcolm Harris's writing, and felt his own performance rise to the rhythms of the play.

The scene with Lesley-Jane started. Everyone knew the climax was approaching. Lesley-Jane looked strained and peaky and her performance was once again subdued. The audience was silent, waiting. They seemed to know when the tragedy of the previous night had occurred, and had maybe come to the theatre in such numbers in the vague hope that they might get a repeat showing.

This thought came into Charles's already overcrowded mind, and he found himself looking off into the wings, whence the fatal shot had come.

He was surprised how little he could see. The brightness of the light on stage made it difficult for him to focus, and a large spot, positioned to give the illusion of daylight from a window of the set, left the recesses of the wings in obscurity. Charles could not even see the A.S.M. who was reading his lines, though he knew the youth would be keeping him in view to watch for signs of difficulty. To be seen from the stage on the O.P. side, a person would have to stand very close to the edge of the set.

Lesley-Jane Decker had seen someone or something in the wings the previous night and it had made her scream. He felt sure of that. It wasn't the sight of Michael Banks falling that had set her off. She had looked off stage and then screamed.

Charles decided he must talk to her when the opportunity arose.

But the thoughts of detection were fatal to his concentration. He lost the line again and, though he tried to disguise the lapse with a dramatic move, he feared he had broken the tension of the scene.

But it was a good scene and, by the time he got to the Hooded Owl speech, he was back on course. He felt very emotional, caught up in his own acting and awareness of the speech's significance from the night before. The emotion and power built through the lines.

As he turned to face the glass case, he felt every eye in the theatre on him.

". . . This stuffed bird has always been in the room. Imagine it had perception, a memory to retain our follies. Oh God, the weakness that these walls have witnessed! And this bird has lived through it all, has seen it all, impassively, in silence."

He reached for the case and took it in both hands.

"Well, I'm not going to be spied on any longer!"

He dashed the Hooded Owl down on to the middle of the stage, where it shattered satisfyingly.

In the audience no one breathed. He had them exactly where every actor who ever lived wants his public, watching his every movement, letting him dictate their lives for a little moment.

He knew the speech had worked.

Probably it was because of what had happened in the play at that point on the previous night.

But was perhaps a little part of its success, he dared to hope, because he had done it rather well?

It was only when he got back to the Star Dressing Room after the performance that Charles fully took in its luxurious appointments. It was wallpapered in a pleasing pattern and the chairs were painted gold with red velvet seats. There was an attractive screen in one corner. On the make-up table was that incredible rarity backstage—a telephone. And, as if that wasn't enough, the dressing room turned out to be *two* rooms. Through a door was another little compartment, with a *bed* and a *fridge*.

Charles kept looking round for the room's occupant. He still couldn't believe it was him.

Members of cast rushed in and out, throwing their arms round him effusively. It wasn't what usually happened to him after a performance. To his fury, he found he was crying.

Paul Lexington came in. "Terrific, Charles. Really bloody marvellous!" And he thrust a brown paper parcel into his hands.

It felt like a bottle. It was a bottle. And a better bottle than he had dared hope. A large bottle of Bell's whisky.

Charles realised that he had previously underestimated the young producer's sensitivity.

"You like one now, Paul?"

"No, thanks. Look, I've booked us all into the Italian place round the corner. Sort of thank you. See you there as soon as you can make it."

"Terrific. Thank you." Charles poured himself a large slug of whisky and downed it. It didn't touch anything till his stomach, whence it sent out radiance.

Then he noticed that there was an envelope on his make-up table. Addressed "Charles Paris", he was sure it hadn't been there at the interval.

He tore the envelope open, his mind full of various pleasing conjectures. The letter lived up to none of them, though its contents were not unpleasing.

The notepaper was headed with a Knightsbridge address.

Dear Charles,

I gather that you are taking over tonight from poor Micky. Just wanted to drop you a note to say break a leg and all those other theatrical clichés. You are very brave to step into the breach.

Be nice to see you some time. If you'd like to meet up for a drink or something, do give me a call on the above number.

All the best for tonight

Dottie

Try as he might, he could not read the letter without feeling sexual overtones. Just as when she had spoken to him, the invitation seemed overt. And, in the heightened mood brought on by the success of his performance, it was an invitation he felt inclined to take up.

106

On the other hand, it was strange . . . If he was reading it right, it was hardly the behaviour of a recently widowed woman, particularly one who had lost her husband in such dramatic circumstances. Even if they lived apart, surely . . . Perhaps he was fantasising.

He looked at it again, searching for another reading. He found one, but didn't like it, because it hinged on the word "brave". Micky Banks had been shot dead on stage. Might his successor be "brave" because he was laying himself open to the same fate . . . ?

There was a tap at the door. "Come in."

He saw Frances in the mirror. With an instinctive and depressingly familiar reflex, he pushed Dottie's letter under a towel and turned to greet his wife.

"Good God. Were you out front?"

She nodded. "Charles, you were wonderful."

Her arms were round his neck and her lips against his. Unwelcome tears threatened again to expose him for a big softie.

"Oh, Frances."

"Charles."

They swayed together. Very together.

"You really did it. I knew you could. I've always known you could be much better than the sort of parts you usually play. And tonight you proved it."

"Thank you very much, Frances." He meant it. She was a shrewd lady and not over-generous with praise, so, when it came, he appreciated it the more.

"I was really proud of you tonight, Charles."

He felt embarrassed. "Would you like a drink or . . . ?"

"No, thanks."

"We're all going out for a meal. Now I come to think of it, I haven't eaten anything all day. Nothing's passed my lips since that cup of tea this morning."

"What about your old friend?" Frances pointed to the bottle of Bell's.

"I've only just had one slug of that. Five minutes ago." Again his mind was clouded by the heresy that had struck him after the first night in Taunton. "Do you realise, Frances . . ." he said slowly, "I did that performance tonight without having had a single drink all day. . . ? And it was all right, wasn't it?"

"It was wonderful."

"Good Lord." He had to sit down because of the shock.

"Perhaps." But the shock stayed with him. He had to have a long swig of Bell's to shift it. "Well, what about coming out for a meal with all of us?"

"No. Thank you, Charles. I have eaten and I've got to get back. Anyway, this'll really be a cast thing. I'll just be out of place."

He didn't attempt to deny it. Frances had been married to an actor long enough to know what she was talking about.

"Well, look, we must meet soon."

"I'd like that. Incidentally, I rang Juliet today."

"Oh yes?"

"To tell her what you were doing. You know, taking on this part. She was very proud."

"Oh." It had never occurred to him that his daughter might be proud of him.

"She and Miles'd love to see you."

"Oh, I'd love to see them."

"I'm going down Sunday week. It's my half-term. I don't know if you'd like to . . ."

"Oh. Oh well, yes, I might. I'll give you a buzz."

"Fine," said Frances without excessive confidence. Charles's buzzes were not notorious for their reliability. "And, incidentally, what I suspected is true."

"Ah," Charles observed knowingly. But there was no point in pretending with Frances. "Er, what did you suspect?"

"Juliet's pregnant again."

"Oh, is she?"

The theory that Charles Paris might be a better actor without alcohol was not put to the test any further that night. Like all good scientists, he knew that one should not rush experiments, so a great deal of Italian red wine and a good few Sambucas were consumed before he finally tottered into a taxi and gave the driver (with some difficulty) his address.

The meal had been fun. He had needed to wind down after the spiralling tensions of the day, and once again he felt the company warmth and support that had sustained him through the day. Meals after shows, with a company who all got on, Charles found, were the moments he most enjoyed of being an actor. They did not happen that often—at least the meals happened, but not often with such unanimity of good humour. But when they did they were wonderful, and some of Charles's happiest memories were of Italian or Chinese or Indian restaurants after hours in quiet provincial towns.

In spite of the alcohol and the fatigues of the day, he did not feel sleepy when he got back to his bed-sitter. His mind was too full. Every time he lay down, some new thought or memory would excite him, and he would start walking round the room.

He knew he should sleep. The next day was Saturday, which meant two performances, and he was already nearly on his knees from exhaustion. But sleep didn't come and round about half past three he realised it wasn't going to come.

So he made a cup of coffee (realising, sensibly for once, that he'd had enough alcohol), and sat down in the low upholstered chair with wooden arms that was one of the room's few comforts.

It didn't take long before he was thinking of Michael Banks's death. Something about it disturbed him—not the obvious facts of its shock and tragedy—but some discordant element, something that didn't ring true. His dormant detective instinct was stirring.

For the moment he set aside the obvious solution. Say Alex Household *hadn't* murdered the star, then who else might have had motive and opportunity to do it?

Michael Banks had been a man who inspired love, but even so Charles could produce quite a list of people who might have had a grudge against him. Whether any of the grudges was strong enough to justify murder was another consideration he put on one side for the time being.

Paul Lexington resented the money he was having to pay to Michael Banks since Bobby Anscombe had backed out of the production. His sums worked better with the star out of the way.

Malcolm Harris had been furious with Michael Banks for, as he mistakenly thought, making arbitrary cuts in the author's precious speeches.

George Birkitt resented Michael Banks's precedence over himself.

Dottie Banks might have resented her husband's apparent liaison with Lesley-Jane Decker and killed him out of jealousy.

Lesley-Jane Decker, if she was having an affair with Michael Banks, might have turned against him because he tried to break it off or committed one of the million other offences which men can commit against women with whom they are having affairs.

Valerie Cass might have resented Michael Banks's affair with her precious daughter, either because of his age or because she was just jealous.

That seemed to be it, as far as motives were concerned, and, even to produce that list, he'd had to scrape the barrel a bit.

And some of the people who had motives were excluded from suspicion by lack of opportunity. Lesley-Jane Decker had been on stage at the time of the shooting, so, unless she had brought in a hired killer, she seemed to be in the clear.

Dottie Banks had been sitting in the auditorium, so she was exonerated, with the same proviso.

The remaining four had all been backstage at the relevant time, or could have been, but the motives Charles had managed to dredge up for them didn't survive close scrutiny.

Paul Lexington had too much at stake in the production to take the risk of being discovered as a murderer. And, although he had benefited from the publicity surrounding the death and from the cheapness of the star's replacement, he would also have benefited from Michael Banks's drawing power, had he survived. No, too fanciful to consider him in the role of murderer. He might well be guilty of swindling people, but not of shooting them.

Valerie Cass's motive seemed pretty feeble, too. She might well be capable of attacking someone who threatened Lesley-Jane or the girl's career, which she lived with such fierce vicariousness, but there was no sign that Michael Banks did represent any such threat. On the contrary she seemed rather to welcome Lesley-Jane's attachment. She liked the reflected glory of her daughter's being with such a famous star, and thought it could do nothing but good for the girl's future in the theatre. Had it been Alex Household who had been shot, the situation would have been different, because she so patently disapproved of him, but with Michael Banks as the victim, it was difficult to cast her in the role of murderer.

And to think of George Birkitt in that light was just ridiculous. He resented Michael Banks, but no more than he resented anyone else more famous than he was. He was far too lazy (and not bright enough) to plan a murder.

Malcolm Harris was a slightly different proposition. He was clearly not a very stable person. He was absolutely obsessed by his play, and might regard what he saw as wanton tampering with it as a threat to his whole personality. But he was also a great admirer of Michael Banks, who was his dream casting for the role, and, unless one introduced very tortuous psychopathology, for him to murder the star was utterly unlikely.

And for any of these suspects to have done it, one had to posit a very unlikely set of circumstances. They would have had to know where

110

Alex's gun was in the Green Room, they would have had to run the risk of being observed on the O.P. side of the stage when they committed the murder . . . This last was not such a great risk, because most of the stage staff were needed on the Prompt Side at that point in the play for a forthcoming scene change.

But there was one witness the potential murderer could not avoid, and that was the main suspect. No one could have gone into the O.P. wings and shot Michael Banks without being seen by Alex Household.

At that point all theories of alternative murderers fell apart.

Alex Household had a history of mental instability and paranoia. He had recently had a starring part and a new girl-friend, both of which he saw as part of a new start in his life, taken away by Michael Banks.

He had voiced threats against the star, and that very evening showed signs of starting another breakdown.

He had been sitting all evening in exactly the spot from which the gun had been fired. He was still there right up until the moment of the shooting, because Michael Banks, who didn't know his lines, was still delivering them correctly and therefore still having them fed to him.

The gun that had shot the star was Alex Household's gun, on which, Charles had discovered at dinner that evening, the police had found no fingerprints but those of the owner.

And, if anyone needed further proof of guilt after that, Alex Household had run away from the scene of the crime. And, in spite of police demands that he give himself up and intensive searches, he was still at large.

Anyone who tried to prove Alex Household didn't do it, when faced with all that evidence, needed his head examined.

Oh, sod it. It was five o'clock. Charles went back on his resolution and poured himself a large Bell's. Maybe lull himself into a little sleep. All this thought of death was unsettling him.

He remembered the words of Tate Wilkinson, the eighteenth-century actor-manager. "No actor can speak of death without a bottle in his hand."

Charles Paris knew what he meant.

CHAPTER TWELVE

THE SATURDAY'S performances of *The Hooded Owl* were not very good. In the euphoria of getting through the first night, Charles had forgotten how much concentration that effort had taken, and found it difficult to get back the rhythm of his lines with the A.S.M. The sleepless night and the excesses which it had incorporated did not help, either.

And the rest of the cast were less altruistically supportive. They too were suffering from exhaustion after recent events, and had less energy to carry Charles; their main concern was just to keep themselves going. They had all reached that stage following a crisis, which can often be more difficult than the crisis itself, when it is no longer a matter of one superhuman push, but husbanding resources for an indeterminately prolonged period of stress. There was huge relief when the curtain fell on the Saturday night performance. No talk of going out for meals then, everyone rushed off to their respective homes, grateful for the knowledge that they would not have to be back in the Variety Theatre until the "half" on the Monday evening.

There was still no news of Alex Household, though police investigations were being vigorously pursued. Either he had gone to ground very effectively and was in hiding, or—and this was a rumour that spread increasingly amongst the cast—he had killed himself. The more days went by, the more likely it became that the end of the police search would be the discovery of a corpse. It was a thought that depressed Charles considerably.

He slept a lot of the Sunday and Monday and, when awake, just mooched about his bed-sitter in the gloom that inevitably followed moments of high excitement.

He thought of ringing Frances, but something deterred him. She had spoken of meeting the following weekend and going down to Juliet's. That possibly meant that she had something else on this weekend. Or would be busy sorting things out at school with the run-up to half-term.

He didn't feel up to the mildest of rebuffs from her; he seemed to have got back to a relationship like an adolescent infatuation, reading rejection in the most innocent of her actions.

His mood also deterred him from ringing Dottie Banks. It was something he still intended to do, but he felt he should be at a peak of confidence to arrange such an encounter.

Still, the rest did him good, and the performance on the Monday evening was better. It was well received by a fairly small house. About a third full. The publicity of Michael Banks's death had now been replaced in the public's mind with news of fresh disasters, and the show was running on its own impetus. The Variety Theatre's position off the main West End beat, the obscurity of the play, and the (*pace* George Birkitt) lack of star names—all the elements which pessimists had predicted would work against the show—were now beginning to take their toll.

Paul Lexington seemed, as ever, undaunted by the small audience. It was Monday night, he said, and that was always bad. The following for this kind of play would build up by word-of-mouth, he insisted. The coach-parties hadn't started to come in yet. And he was going to give a rocket to Show-Off, whose performance on the publicity front had been absolutely dismal. Get another burst of publicity in the second week, and the show would be fine. Every production went through troughs.

As ever, he sounded terribly plausible, and Charles was as willing as all the rest of the cast to believe what he said. How true it all was, Charles didn't wish to investigate. And how the show was now funded, how tightly Paul Lexington was running his budget, what his break-even percentage of audience was, indeed how much of the audience was made up of paying theatre-goers and how much of free seats; all these were questions to which he knew he was unlikely to get answers.

All they could do was work from day to day, from performance to performance, and through the second week, Charles started to feel his confidence in the part building up again. The play settled down with its new cast. The size of the audience didn't increase noticeably, but the faithful few who did turn up seemed appreciative.

He even got another nice review. Obviously there had been no notices after the first night, and few of the critics of the major papers would have had time, let alone interest, to give the play a second viewing; but a North London local paper with a weekly deadline had sent along its critic on the Monday of the second week, and their review appeared on the Thursday.

The significant sentence read as follows: "The part of the father, played by an actor unfamiliar to me, Charles Paris, grows in stature through the evening until the powerfully climactic scene of confrontation with his daughter."

It was not, of course, unambiguous praise. Indeed, it could have been read merely as appreciation of Malcolm Harris's writing; it was the part, after all, not the acting, which was said to grow in stature. And, to the cynically analytical mind which Charles usually applied to praise, the review could be read to mean that the part grew in stature until the powerfully climactic scene of confrontation with his daughter, at which point, in the hands of this actor, it diminished considerably.

But, on the whole, he thought it was good. Like all actors with reviews, he checked through it for quotability, and decided that, with only slight injustice to the meaning, and the excision of a comma, he could come up with the very serviceable sentence, "Charles Paris grows in stature through the evening."

He even wondered if he ought to suggest to Paul Lexington that that sentence was put on a hoarding outside the theatre, but didn't quite have the nerve. The producer had been satisfied with snipping out from the same review the words, "a thoroughly solid evening's entertainment", to join the other encomiums that guarded the Variety's portals.

(These others, incidentally, demonstrated once again Paul Lexington's very personal definition of truth and his skill in the use of small print. Since he hadn't got any London press reviews, he had used the Taunton ones, and artfully disguised their provenance. Thus the passer-by would observe in large letters the exhortation, "I urge everyone to go and see *The Hooded Owl* now!—*Times*". He would have to go very close indeed to the hoarding to read the word "*Taunton*" between "now!" and "*Times*".

In the same way, the "*Observer*", which acclaimed "an evening of theatrical magic", was the "*Quantock Observer*"; and the "*Mail*", who had "rarely been so entertained" was the "*Western Mail*".

The cheekiest of the lot was actually from a London newspaper. "One of the greatest dramas in the history of the British Theatre" was, as its by-line claimed, from "*The Daily Telegraph*"; it had come, however, not from the Arts page, but from the front page description of Michael Banks's murder.

There were no flies on Paul Lexington.

Charles cut out and kept his probably-nice review. He never kept bad ones. That was not just vanity. He always found that, while he could

114

never exactly fix the wording of the good ones, the bad remained indelibly printed on his brain, accurate to the last comma.

Though over thirty years had passed, he could still remember how his first major role for the Oxford University Dramatic Society had been greeted by an undergraduate critic (who, incidentally, later became a particularly malevolent Minister of Health and Social Security):

"Charles Paris had a brave stab at the part, but unfortunately it did not survive his attack."

On the Wednesday matinée, when the house was minimal and so was the cast's concentration, Charles came rather unstuck with his deaf-aid.

To be honest, it wasn't his fault. Or it wasn't *completely* his fault. He got fed the wrong line.

Inevitably, it was in the Hooded Owl speech, the play's focus for either triumph or disaster. Charles had just turned to face the glass case, having made the analogy of the Hooded Owl and God. The line he should have received next was, "Why not? This stuffed bird has always been in the room." But, unfortunately, what the A.S.M. read to him was, "Why not? This bird has always been stuffed in this room."

And, even more unfortunately, that was the line Charles repeated.

The audience probably didn't notice anything wrong; their reactions were so minimal, anyway, that it hardly mattered. But Lesley-Jane certainly did, and she started to giggle. That, and the mild hysteria that a tiny audience always engenders, got Charles going too, and the pair of them were almost paralysed by laughter. It was what actors call a total "corpse", and, although they managed to get through to the end of the play, any tension they might have built up was dissipated.

The lapse was duly noted by the Stage Manager and no one was surprised to be summoned on stage at the "half" for the evening show, and receive a dressing-down from the Company Manager.

"You're all meant to be professionals," Wallas Ward berated them petulantly, "and this sort of behaviour is unforgivable. We already have our problems with this show, and we're at a very pivotal point. If we are to survive in the West End, we have to guarantee that *every* performance is up to scratch. Nothing brings a show's reputation down quicker than the rumour going round the business that the cast has started sending it up. You really should know better."

Charles owned up, like a naughty schoolboy. "Sorry, it was my fault. I got fed the wrong line."

"Well, you should have been concentrating on what you were saying.

115

You are meant to think, not just relay the lines like some glorified loudspeaker."

"Yes, I know. I'm sorry. Lapse of concentration. Won't happen again."

"It'd better not. I think you ought to be off the deaf-aid by now."

"What?" Charles was very taken aback.

"Well, you are going to learn the lines at some point, aren't you?"

"Oh, I . . . er . . . I hadn't really thought about it." He hadn't. Now he had sorted out the technique of using the deaf-aid, he found it wonderfully relaxing. The strain of remembering the lines was removed, and he could enjoy the acting. It hadn't occurred to him that at some point his life-support system would be taken away.

"*I* think you should be off the deaf-aid now," asserted Wallas Ward righteously. "But Paul says wait a bit, no hurry, and it's his decision."

"Right, well, I'll wait till I hear from him."

"And, in the meantime, let us have no repetition of this afternoon's disgusting display of amateurism."

Very good, Wallas, yes, Wallas, certainly, Wallas, said all the cast, touching their forelocks in mock-abasement.

"Maurice Skellern Personal Management."

"Still holding out for the twenty per cent, I see, Maurice."

"Charles, one has to pay for personal service in this day and age. It's the same all over the board, you know."

"Humph."

"Well, and how's the show going?"

"Oh, thank you for asking. I take it that question is an example of your Personal Management, the individual care you lavishly bestow on your clients."

"Exactly, Charles."

"Listen, Maurice, we last spoke nearly a fortnight ago. Since then, not only has the show opened in the West End, but also I, your client, have taken over the leading part. And during that time, what kind of 'individual care' have I received? Not even a lousy telephone call. I always have to end up ringing you."

"I'm never sure where you are, Charles."

"Rubbish. You could always find me if you tried."

"I think you're being very hurtful, Charles. I spend all day beavering away on your behalf and—"

"Oh, damn it, Maurice, can't you—"

116

"That's very good, Charles, very good." Wheezes of laughter wafted down the telephone line.

"What?"

"Beavering—damn it. Very good."

"Listen, Maurice, as I say I am now playing the lead in this show, and I think it is about time you sorted out some deal on the money I get for doing it."

"Now, Charles, if you would calm down a moment and allow me to get a word in, I would be able to inform you that I have already negotiated just such a deal for you."

"Then why the hell didn't you tell me?"

"Because the details have only recently been finalised with Paul Lexington."

"Well, when did you ring him?"

"He rang me, actually."

"When?"

"Yesterday."

"And I suppose that was the first you knew of my taking over the part?"

"It was, as it happens."

"I don't bloody believe it. Your office must have a great pile of sand in it instead of a desk, so that you can keep your head buried all bloody day."

"Now, Charles . . . An agent's job is difficult enough without his clients being offensive."

"All right. Tell me what the deal is."

Charles had devoted considerable thought to this subject. He knew that he wasn't the most eminent actor in the world, but he still knew that nobody played a starring part in the West End for peanuts. He had to be on three hundred and fifty a week minimum, surely? Maybe a bit more. Maybe a lot more.

"Paul Lexington was very fair on the phone, I thought, very fair."

"Oh yes?"

"What he said was . . ."

"Yes?"

" . . . that he'd continue to pay your existing contract—"

"But that's only a hundred and fifty a week."

"Wait, wait. But, on top of that, he was prepared to pay a supplement."

"Oh good."

"Because you are actually playing the part."

"I certainly am."

"A supplement of ten pounds for each performance you do."

"Ten pounds! But that's nothing!"

"It's quite generous for an understudy."

"But I'm not an understudy. This isn't the part which I was understudying, anyway. And I am actually playing the part."

"Not according to Paul Lexington."

"What do you mean?"

"According to him, you are acting as understudy. And, in a few weeks when he sees how business is going, he will make the decision as to whether to confirm you in the part or to recast."

"Good God."

"As I say, I thought it was very fair. I mean, considering your stature in the business."

"Thank you very much," said Charles dully.

"I pushed him up, you know. He only wanted to give you eight pounds a performance, but I pushed him up."

"Terrific, Maurice."

But the sarcasm was wasted. "Good, I thought you'd see it my way. And now perhaps you understand what I mean by Personal Management."

"Oh yes, I think I do."

"Good. Well, nice to talk to you."

"Hmm. I don't suppose your Personal Management and 'individual care' would actually extend to coming along to see the show, would it?"

"Oh now, Charles . . . I spend all day in the office slaving away on your behalf. Surely you don't want me to give up my evenings too. Do you . . . ?"

Michael Banks's death niggled away at Charles like a hole in the tooth. He had done all the sums, and he knew only one answer fitted, but still something snagged. There seemed little doubt that Alex was the murderer, but Charles felt somehow he owed it to his friend to isolate the element about the case that was worrying him.

So, just before the "half" on the Thursday night, he knocked on Lesley-Jane Decker's dressing room door.

She was dressed in a silk kimono and lying on the daybed when he went in. Her face was scoured of street make-up, prior to the application of her stage make-up. The result was pale and sickly, stress lines showing

118

how much she would look like her mother in a few years' time. It was brought home to Charles for the first time how much of a strain the last weeks must have been for a girl of her age. To have broken off one affair and started another, then to have witnessed the shooting of her new lover by the old one, was quite a lot to take. He knew some actresses, hard-boiled as eight-minute eggs, who would have revelled in the situation, casting themselves as *femmes fatales* with enormous relish. But Lesley-Jane didn't seem the type. Her sophistication was paper-thin, and underneath she was just a very young, and probably over-protected, girl.

She made no attempt to move when he came in, just lay there looking vulnerable. Nor did she say anything beyond "Hello, Charles." Her champagne bubble was distinctly flat.

"Tired out?" he asked solicitously.

"Shattered."

"Yes, it's been tough for all of us. Doing eight shows a week is enough, without all this other business . . ."

"Yes." She looked at him, curious as to why he was there. But not that curious; she seemed too tired to be very interested.

"I wanted to talk about Michael's death," he began bluntly.

"Ah." Even this didn't animate her much.

"I'm sorry to go through it all again, but there's something about it that seems odd to me."

"What?"

"Well, that's the trouble. You see, I don't know. There's just something that doesn't seem right about it."

"I don't think murder's often right," she observed with a touch more spirit.

"No. By definition it isn't. But listen, we both witnessed that murder. I was out front, and it was pretty horrible from there. From where you were standing, it must have been . . ."

She gulped, forcing back nausea, and nodded.

"But what interests me, what I wanted to ask you, is about how you reacted."

"I screamed, didn't I? I can't remember very well, but I thought I . . ."

"Yes, you screamed all right. It was *when* you screamed that interests me."

"When?"

"Yes. What happened was this: Micky stopped getting the lines,

119

turned round in confusion, then presumably saw someone in the wings pointing a gun at him. He said 'Put it down. You mustn't do that to me' or something and then he was shot."

Lesley-Jane nodded. She wasn't enjoying the re-creation of the shock.

"But you didn't scream then."

"Didn't I? I can't remember. It was all confused . . ."

"No, you didn't scream until you looked off into the wings."

"Delayed shock, I suppose. I couldn't believe what had happened to Micky straight away, I didn't even *know* what had happened to him."

"But when you looked into the wings you *did* know. And you also knew who had done it. And then you screamed."

"Yes. I suppose it brought it home to me."

"And who did you see in the wings?"

She looked at him as if he were daft. "Well, Alex, of course."

He didn't know what he had been expecting, but he felt very disappointed. Something inside had been hoping against all logic for a different answer. He didn't know what, just anything that would settle the unease he felt about the death.

"What exactly did you see?"

"I've been through all this with the police . . ."

"I know. I'm sorry. It's just . . . I wasn't backstage for all the police inquiries, and I really would like to know," he appealed pathetically.

"All right. I saw Alex. He was very near the edge of the set . . ."

Must have been. Charles knew how impenetrable the shadows were in the wings.

"He looked over his shoulder at me, our eyes met for a split-second, then he rushed off and I screamed. I suppose it was the expression on his face that made me scream."

"Because it made you realise what he'd done?"

"Yes, I think he'd only just realised himself. His face was . . . I don't know . . . it was full of fear."

"Was the gun in his hand?"

"The police asked me that, too, and honestly, I just can't remember. I didn't notice his hands."

"Was he wearing his jacket?"

"Again I just don't know. All I seemed to see was his face—or maybe just his eyes. I can't get them out of my mind even now. Those eyes full of terror. I felt awful, as if I had hurt him. He was always very unstable, you know."

"Yes." Charles reckoned he could take advantage of her lethargic state to push a bit further. "I suppose, of course, you *had* hurt him . . ."

"You mean by going off with Micky?"

Charles nodded.

"Yes. I suppose so. It didn't really seem like that at the time. I mean Micky just seemed so nice, so friendly and, in a strange way, so lonely. Going and having a few meals with him didn't seem evil or furtive in any way. Somehow it was difficult to feel anything was *wrong* with Micky around."

He knew what she meant. Michael Banks's effortless charm no doubt carried through into his romantic life.

"And it was just a few meals . . . ?"

He had hoped she wouldn't notice the impertinence, but she coloured and began angrily, "I don't see that that's any business of yours . . . but yes, it was."

"Whereas with Alex . . . ?"

"That again is no business of yours . . ."

"Come on, we were all in Taunton together . . . It certainly had the look, to the impartial observer, of a full-blown affair."

"All right, yes. But I had wanted to break it off after Taunton. It was getting awkward, even before I met Micky."

"Awkward?" Charles fed gently.

"Alex was so strange. The more time I spent with him, the stranger he seemed to be. All his mystical religion thing, his faddishness about food, his belief in being close to nature, following nature . . . all that appealed to me at first. It was so unlike anything I had come across before. He was so unlike any of the people I had met before . . ."

Certainly unlike the nice middle-class friends of Mr. and Mrs. Decker, Charles imagined.

"But, after a time, I began to see all his ideas as sort of odd, not charming eccentricities, but . . . you know, symptoms."

"Symptoms of what?"

"Of his mental state. I knew he had had the breakdown and at first I didn't mind. I thought, oh, he just needs someone who really loves him and will look after him . . ."

"And you thought you could supply that want?"

She nodded. "I thought we really would make a new start, that I would sort of . . . make him blossom."

She blushed, as if aware of the cliché she was using. Charles wondered how many naïve young girls had got caught in messy affairs with older

121

men from the belief that they could bring new love into their lives and "make them blossom".

"But," he prompted.

"But I came to realise that it's all very well gambolling about the countryside feeling at one with nature, but people don't change completely. We couldn't go on pretending that the first forty-seven years of Alex's life hadn't happened. And, as soon as I realised that, as soon as I thought about his breakdown, I started to worry, I started to see just how unstable he still was. I started to be afraid."

"Afraid of what?"

"Afraid that he would do something . . . well, something like he did do last week."

Charles nodded slowly. "And what about now? Where do you think he is now?"

Tears came to her eyes. "I think he'll have killed himself."

Charles nodded again. It seemed depressingly likely.

Further conversation was prevented by the door opening, unknocked, to admit Valerie Cass. She was smartly dressed in a fawn trouser suit and seemed in high spirits.

"Hello, darling, I've brought you some—oh, hello." This last was to acknowledge Charles, whom she looked at for a moment with suspicion.

"Charles just dropped in to wish me luck," Lesley-Jane supplied hastily.

Don't worry, Valerie, I'm not another older man sniffing round your precious daughter. Which, considering the fate of the last two, is perhaps just as well.

As a matter of fact, I don't really fancy her. I used to, I think, but since I met you and saw what she was likely to turn into, I seem to have gone off her. In spite of your excellent state of preservation, Valerie Cass, I'm afraid there's something about you that doesn't appeal to me.

Valerie cut short further interior monologue by gracing him with a smile and saying, "I just brought Lesley-Jane some home-made soup for the interval. She doesn't eat properly. I keep saying she should eat little and often, but the young don't listen. You have a daughter, don't you, Charles?"

"Yes, I don't see her that often."

She leapt on this, a useful confirmation of one of her pet theories. "Yes, as usual no doubt it's the woman who's left to take care of things. Poor Frances, I do feel for her."

"My daughter is twenty-eight, you know, quite capable of looking

122

after herself without her parents breathing down her neck all the time." He just managed to resist adding, "Yours is twenty, and I would have thought the same went for her too."

Sensing that something of the sort might be going through his mind, Lesley-Jane interposed, "We were just talking about Micky's death."

"Oh, what a terrible tragedy." Valerie Cass made an elaborate gesture, reminding Charles once again what a bad actress she had been. "It was so awful for all of us. Lesley-Jane was desolated, but desolated. I was so glad that I was up here when she came off stage. If ever there was a moment when a girl needed her mother, that was it. And to sort of protect her during all that police interrogation. I was just glad I could be of help."

She smiled beatifically. She seemed to have new confidence in her hold over her daughter. It's an ill wind, thought Charles. Micky Banks's death and Alex Household's disappearance were tragedies, but at least they had removed possible rivals for Valerie's daughter's affections.

And Lesley-Jane didn't seem to mind her mother's renewed take-over. In her shocked lethargy, she seemed content to let Valerie run around after her and do everything for her.

But Michael Banks's memory remained sacred. Perhaps, after all, Valerie hadn't resented him, grateful for his reflected glory. That seemed to be the case from what she said next. "Poor, dear Micky . . . Such a terrible tragedy. And just when he and Lesley-Jane were getting . . . close. Oh, I know some people would say it was May and December, but I thought it was a lovely relationship. He just seemed so delighted, so *rejuvenated* to meet my little baby. What might have been . . ."

She sighed the sort of sigh that drama teachers spend three years eradicating from their students. Lesley-Jane, perhaps from long experience of having her mother going on about her or perhaps just from exhaustion, did not seem to be listening.

"Oh yes, I think Lesley-Jane could have mixed with some very eminent people. She is just the sort of girl to stimulate the artistic temperament. Don't you agree, Charles?"

Charles, who shared G. K. Chesterton's opinion that the artistic temperament is a disease which afflicts amateurs, grunted. He could well believe that Lesley-Jane could stimulate male lust; but he found her mother's visions of her, launched in society as a kind of professional Laura to a series of theatrical Petrarchs, a little fanciful.

"Mind you, at the same age, I myself . . ." she blushed, " . . . was not without admirers in the . . . world of the arts. If I hadn't been trapped by marriage so young . . . who knows what might have been . . .? Though of course I wasn't *half* as attractive as Lesley . . ."

This was said in a voice expecting contradiction, which Charles wilfully withheld.

CHAPTER THIRTEEN

THE CONFIDENCE to ring Dottie Banks, absent over the weekend, came after the Friday's performance. The show had gone well, and Charles felt his acting had matched it. There was even a slight swagger in his stride as he entered the Star Dressing Room. (In spite of his enduring understudy status and certain representations that George Birkitt had made to the Company Manager, Charles was still in there.)

Once inside, he saw that great perk, the telephone, and remembered Dottie's note. He also remembered that he'd said he'd ring Frances about the possibility of going down to Miles and Juliet's on the Sunday, but decided to do that the next morning.

He dialled Dottie's number, trying not to dwell on thoughts of the times Michael Banks must have done the same from the same phone.

No, she didn't mind his ringing so late. And yes, she was glad to hear from him. And yes, she had meant what she had said in her note, that it'd be nice to get together for a chat and . . . things. And why didn't he drop round to her flat in Hans Crescent for a drink after the show tomorrow?

Charles conceded that he would be free, and graciously accepted the invitation.

Drinks with strange women after the show fitted well into the fantasy of himself as the big West End star that the night's performance had engendered.

Even as he thought it, he couldn't help remembering that West End stars tended to be paid a bit more than he was getting with his humble understudy-plus-supplement deal. He really must have a word with the company Equity representative about that contract. Surely Equity wouldn't approve it.

On the other hand, since his agent had accepted the terms so avidly, he thought there might be problems in getting them changed.

Still, there was plenty of time to sort that out. His main priority was Dottie Banks. When he thought of their forthcoming encounter, he felt the guilty excitement of a schoolboy sneaking into the cinema to see an "X" Certificate movie.

The block of flats in Hans Crescent was expensive and discreet. The porter who rang up to Mrs. Banks and directed Charles to her flat was also no doubt expensive, and would have been discreet if he had refrained from accompanying his directions with a wink. Charles got the impression that perhaps he wasn't the first to have followed this particular route.

The Dottie Banks who opened the flat door was looking expensive; as to her discretion, he would no doubt soon find out. The black satin trousers, the fine black silk shirt and the black lace brassiere which was meant to show through it; they too were expensive. And just about discreet.

"Charles, how nice to see you." She threw her arms round his neck and kissed him on the lips, enveloping him in discreetly expensive perfume. "Come in and have a drink."

The same adjectives which had applied to everything else applied to the flat. Charles was unused to moving in circles where interior designers were used; most of his friends just accumulated clutter and wielded emulsion brushes when things got too tatty; but he recognised the genuine article when he saw it. And he had to admit it was well done.

There was a great deal of Michael Banks memorabilia about. Photographs, framed posters, the odd award statuette. Whatever the nature of their relationship, it was clear that husband and wife had shared the same flat.

Charles was looking at a film still of Banks in one of his most famous roles as the captain of a doomed frigate, when Dottie came back from the kitchen with a bottle of champagne.

"You open this."

"Fine."

"There are some things I always feel men do better than women."

Charles recognised that there would come a point when one found this relentless sexual innuendo irritating. But he knew he hadn't reached that point yet. He put down the still and took the champagne bottle.

"Yes, poor Micky." Dotty Banks sighed. "Poor, poor Micky."

It was said without any sense of tragedy, but with affection.

"It must be pretty awful for you, having lost him." The cork popped and Charles caught the spume in a tall glass.

"Yes, of course I miss him. Not as much as I would have expected, in some ways." Dottie shrugged. "I mean, as a marriage, it wasn't . . . well, it wasn't a marriage in the conventional sense. We got on well, we went around together quite a bit, we were nice to each other, but we always . . . had our own friends."

She looked at him unequivocally, so Charles asked the direct question. "You mean you both had affairs?"

"*I* did."

"But Micky didn't?"

"He had . . . friendships."

"I see." So perhaps Lesley-Jane had been telling the truth in her description of the relationship. Just a few meals.

"What I mean, Charles, is that sex wasn't very high on Micky's list of priorities."

"Ah . . . Well, some people don't have much of a sex-drive," Charles observed fatuously, aware that his own was revving up like mad.

"In Micky's case, he didn't have any."

"Sex-drive?"

"None at all." She shook her head to punctuate the words. "He couldn't do it any more."

"Ah." Charles wasn't sure whether to say he was sorry or not. He didn't know the correct etiquette for replying to a lady who's just told you her recently-murdered husband was impotent.

"This made us, in certain respects, incompatible." Dottie Banks emphasised the obvious by placing her hand on Charles's thigh.

"Ah. Well. Yes. I can see that."

Her fingertips started to move gently up and down. He felt it would soon be the moment to make a move, and her behaviour left him in little doubt as to what sort of move it should be. Indeed, the only question seemed to be whether he should even bother to make a move, or just let her do everything for him.

But, even then, the nagging thought in his mind would not go away. "Dottie, about Micky's death . . ."

"Uhuh." She was now leaning over towards him and breathing very close to his ear. He could feel the hard outline of her breasts against his upper arm.

"Did you think there was anything odd about it?"

"Odd?" she murmured. "Well, no odder than any other murder that takes place on stage during the first night of a new play, when the leading actor is shot dead by his understudy."

"No, I just thought you, knowing Micky so well, might have . . ."

127

"Uhuh." She shook her head, which wobbled the ear she was now nibbling in a way that he found extremely stimulating.

But he still sat still, puzzling, the scene of the murder running like an old movie in his mind.

"Did you come here," mumbled Dottie, very close, "to ask me fatuous questions the police have already been through a hundred times, or for other reasons?"

"For other reasons," he assured her, though deep down he wasn't certain.

"Well then," she said, "are you paralysed?"

His hands, sliding from her hair to her neck and down inside the filmy black blouse, denied the imputation. And, after the two of them had slipped down on to the expensive and discreet rug, the rest of his body also demonstrated its unimpaired mobility.

They moved from the rug to the king-size bed for a second demonstration, after which they lay entwined.

Charles was beginning to wonder whether he actually liked Dottie or not. Her intimacy seemed completely impersonal, and he did rather like being appreciated for himself.

Also, his best efforts did not seem sufficient to her. She didn't say anything, but the way she toyed with him suggested she wanted him to be demonstrating all day like a vacuum cleaner salesman.

At last she realised that, for a little while, her ambitions were vain. She lay back.

"You know you asked if there was anything I thought odd about Micky's death . . ."

"Yes?"

"Well, there was one thing. One tiny thing. So tiny I've only just thought of it."

"What?"

"Well, you know when you spend a lot of time with someone, you get used to how they speak, their mannerisms and so on . . ."

"Yes."

"Just before Micky died, he said something I've never heard him say before."

"What was that?"

"He said, 'Oh Lord!' I've never heard him say that before. 'Oh God,' yes. 'Oh Christ,' many times. But not 'Oh Lord.'"

"Good Lord!"

"No 'Oh Lord!'"

"No, I mean just 'Good Lord!' you know, 'Good Lord!'"

"Hmm?"

"Never mind. Look, Micky never said 'Oh Lord!', but Alex Household was always saying it."

"Oh, was he? Oh well, that explains it."

"How?"

"Alex Household must have said it just before he shot the gun; Micky heard it over the deaf-aid and just repeated it."

"Yes, I suppose so."

Dottie's hands were once again busying themselves.

"Hmm. I don't know, Dottie. I keep wishing there was another solution to this murder."

"How can there be? Alex Household shot Micky. That's the only possible solution."

"Yes, I suppose so," Charles conceded, disgruntled. "I have to admit, it's the best I can come up with."

"Oh, I wouldn't say that."

But Dottie was no longer talking about the murder.

After the third demonstration, Charles said he'd better go, and Dottie, recognising that she'd had all she was getting, took a sleeping pill and let him.

In the taxi back to Hereford Road, Charles felt despicable. Sex without any element of love, or even affection, always had that effect on him.

But this time it seemed worse. It was her taking the sleeping pill that had done it. It had reduced him to the same level, just another anonymous treatment that her body had required.

CHAPTER FOURTEEN

FRANCES REPRESENTED many things for Charles, amongst them a kind of fixed moral standard in his life. To ring her the following morning seemed, therefore, not just a good, but even a *right* idea. Like going to confession (though he had no intention of confessing anything), a bracing moral scour-out.

"Charles. Well, are you coming or not? You've left it late enough."

"Left what late enough?"

"Charles, you remember—Juliet and Miles invited you down for lunch."

"Oh yes, of course."

"You hadn't forgotten, had you?"

"Oh no, I . . . er . . . um . . ."

"Well, are you going to come or not?"

"Um. I hadn't really thought. I . . . er . . ."

"I will be leaving in an hour, Charles. If you're here when I go, you will be coming. If you're not, I will be going on my own."

"Yes, well, of course I—"

"Goodbye, Charles."

Yes, he would go. After the moral squalor of the night before, he needed the redemption of playing at being the respectable husband, father and grandfather. A nice, straight day with the family—that seemed morally appropriate. Though a day with his son-in-law, Miles, could take on certain qualities of a penance.

"Thing is, Pop, you see, that when Mums sells the house, she's going to have a bit of cash in hand."

"Yes, I suppose so." Good God, at what point had Frances lapsed low enough to let Miles call her "Mums"?

"And this is where she's really going to feel the benefit of having someone in the family who knows about insurance." Miles took his mother-in-law's hand confidently. "Aren't you, Mums?" To Charles's amazement, she didn't flinch. "Now, I've got a really exciting little annuity scheme worked out which I think will be just the ticket."

Charles looked across at Miles Taylerson with his customary disbelief. Anyone who could get excited by an annuity scheme must belong to a different species from his own. And yet Miles appeared to have the same complement of arms and legs as he did, the same disposition of eyes, nose and mouth. Maybe, Charles reflected, his son-in-law was the result of some cloning experiment, by which creatures from another planet had created something that looked like a human being, but lacked the essential circuitry of humanity. Maybe one day Miles's head would flip open like a kitchen bin to reveal a tangle of wires and transistors.

"You haven't thought any more about insurance, have you, Pop?"

"No, I think I can honestly say that I haven't." And come to that, what's this "more"? his mind continued silently. It is one of my proudest boasts that I have never thought about insurance and I am convinced that, even under torture, I could resist the temptation.

"I was just thinking that now's a good time. Now you're getting regular money from this West End show, it'd be a good opportunity to put a little aside each week—it needn't be much, but you'd be amazed how it accumulates."

"Thank you. I'm sure if ever the occasion arises when I want advice on insurance, you're the first person I'll come to." Charles thought that wasn't bad. It was the nearest he had ever got to saying something to his son-in-law that was neither untrue nor offensive.

Miles seemed to appreciate it, too. He sat back with a satisfied grin and looked contently around the open-plan hygienic nonentity of his executive sitting room in his executive house on an executive estate in Pangbourne.

His wife seemed to recognise some signal and took up the conversational baton for the next lap. "Incidentally, Daddy, I haven't said how delighted we all are about this West End play. We really hope to get to see it soon, but, you know, things are pretty busy, what with this and that, and the boys . . ."

"Of course." He couldn't help feeling affection for Juliet whenever he looked at her. There was something about the set of her eyes which hadn't changed since she was three years old, when she had been all hugs and trust for her father. He often wondered what it was that had brought about such a change in their relationship. Maybe his walking out on Frances.

He looked across at his wife. She was unaware of his scrutiny, gazing with fondness at the two blond-headed little boys who were shovelling gravy-sodden potato into their mouths, an exercise—and apparently the only one—that kept them silent.

At such moments he knew that he loved Frances, and he could feel the seductions of a conventional marriage, of meals such as this happening every Sunday, of knowing each other's daily news, not always having to catch up on a few months' worth of events. There was a kind of peace about it.

And maybe that peace was not completely beyond his grasp. If he really made an effort, perhaps something could be salvaged.

"No," Juliet continued, "I mean this West End thing is something I can really tell my friends about. It was like when you had that part in *Z-Cars*. Something sort of . . . respectable."

"Thank you," he muttered. Good God, what had happened to Juliet? Her mind had set irrevocably into middle age when she was about ten. Marriage to Miles had only hardened her mental arteries further. The pair of them had just quietly fossilised together.

Julian finished his potatoes and looked gravely round the family gathering. "My penis," he announced, "is as big as the Empire State Building."

His four-year-old twin, Damian, not to be outdone, immediately responded. "And mine penis," he proclaimed, "mine penis is as big as the World Trade Centre."

In the confusion of scolding that followed, Charles reflected that maybe there was hope for the family after all.

Closer acquaintance did nothing to dispel his good impression of his grandsons. After lunch, Juliet, looking peaky and feeling grim, as she had done in the early months of her previous pregnancy, went upstairs to lie down. Frances and Miles went off to the kitchen to do the washing-up (and, no doubt, to talk annuities), leaving Charles to entertain the children.

He found that this was a two-way process. The two little boys were full of ideas for games and, even if most of them ended rather predictably in throwing the sofa cushions at their grandfather, they showed considerable powers of invention.

They were also at the stage when they still found funny voices funny, and Charles had his best audience in years for his Welsh, developed for *Under Milk Wood* ("A production which demonstrated everything the theatre can offer, except talent"—*Nottingham Evening Post*), his Cornish, as used in *Love's Labour's Lost* ("Charles Paris's Costard was about as funny as an obituary notice"—*New Statesman*) and the voice he had used as a Chinese Broker's Man in *Aladdin* ("My watch said that the show only lasted two and a half hours, so I've taken it to be repaired"—*Glasgow Herald*).

Somehow they got into a game of Prisoners. Charles would capture one of the boys and only release him if he said the magic word. The secret of the game was to keep changing the magic word, making it longer and longer and sillier and sillier, in the hope (always realised) that the prisoner would be giggling too much to repeat it. Since, while the prisoner struggled to escape, the unfettered twin would be bombarding his grandfather with cushions, the game was not without hilarity.

Charles clasped his hands round Julian.

"What's the magic word?" Julian gasped.

Woomph, went a cushion from Damian into Charles's face.

"The magic word is—Ongle-bongle-boodle-boodle-boodle."

"Ongle-bongle-boodle-giggle-giggle," Julian repeated, wriggling free.

Damian rushed into the imprisoning arms.

"What's the magic word?"

Woomph, went a cushion from Julian into the back of Charles's neck.

"Nick-picky-wickety-pingle-pang."

"Nicky-picky-diddle-poo-poo." Damian snickered at his daring.

But it wasn't good enough to secure his release.

"No, you have to repeat exactly what I say," insisted Charles.

"No, you have to repeat exactly what I say," repeated Julian, who was catching on. As he said it, he threw a cushion, which went woomph into the side of Charles's head.

"But it's nonsense," objected Damian.

"Even if it's nonsense. You just repeat it like a machine."

"Even if it's nonsense. You just repeat it like a machine," crowed Julian.

"Even if it's nonsense. You just repeat it like a machine," agreed Damian.

"Whatever I say, you have to repeat without thinking."

"Whatever I say, you have to repeat without thinking."

"Whatever I say, you have to repeat without thinking."

Like a light switched on, Charles's mind was suddenly clear. He knew

133

what it was that had struck him as odd about Michael Banks's death. And he knew that Alex Household had not committed the murder.

"Good God! I've got it!" he shouted.

"Good God! I've got it!" shouted Julian.

"Good God! I've got it!" shouted Damian.

He was dialling when Miles and Frances came in from the kitchen.

"Sorry. Hope you don't mind my using the phone."

"Feel free." But Miles didn't look very pleased.

It rang for a long time, and he thought he was going to be out of luck, but eventually the receiver was picked up the other end.

"Hello." Her voice was rather woolly.

"Lesley-Jane, it's me—Charles."

"Charles?"

"Charles Paris."

"Oh." She didn't say what on earth are you ringing for; she put it all into the oh. "Sorry, I was asleep."

"I was glad to find you in. I thought you might be away for the weekend."

"Yes, I was going to my parents, but I . . . I decided not to."

"Listen, I've just thought of something important."

"Oh yes." She sounded belligerent and slightly resentful. Was he going to give her some note on performance, some idea he'd had for a new bit of business in the play? Surely it could wait till tomorrow.

"It's about Alex . . ."

"Oh."

"I've just remembered something he said to me in Taunton . . ."

"Oh yes?"

"He said that one should always sort out a bolt-hole for oneself."

"Well, what does that mean?"

"I thought you might know."

"No idea."

"What I mean is . . . when you were in Taunton, you were fairly discreet about your affair . . . I wondered where . . ."

"Oh, I see."

"You said something last week about 'gambolling in the countryside'. Was there somewhere . . . ?"

"There was, but . . ."

"Where?"

"Do you think . . . ?"

"It's a possibility. I think it's worth investigating."

"You?"

"Why not?"

"I don't know. It just seems vindictive. The idea of bringing him to justice. Still, I suppose you could just tell the police and—"

"I wasn't thinking of bringing him to justice. I was thinking of finding out from him what actually did happen."

"Really?"

"Yes. Tell me where it is."

She told him. "But I've a nasty feeling," she concluded dismally, "that if you do find anything there, it'll just be Alex's body."

He put the phone down and turned round to see the whole family looking at him, open-mouthed. Juliet stood half-way down the stairs, familiarly pale. Charles's mind was working well, making connections fast. He felt confident.

"Frances," he asked, "do you fancy a little trip?"

"Where to?"

"Somerset."

"When?"

"Now."

Miles's face contorted. "Oh really, Pop! It's a hell of a long way. You can't just do things like that, on a whim."

"Why not?" Charles looked at Frances. "It's your half-term, isn't it? Be good to see some real countryside. We could stay in a nice hotel."

"But," objected Juliet, whose every holiday was planned at least six months in advance, "you haven't booked anywhere!"

"What do you say, Frances?"

"All right."

Good old Frances. She wasn't where Juliet got it from either.

It was a nice hotel. On the edge of Exmoor. There was no problem booking. Indeed, after another bad summer for British tourism, they were welcomed with open arms.

They had a drink before dinner sitting in a bay window, watching dusk creep up on Dunkery Beacon. They talked a lot during dinner and then after a couple of brandies, went up to the bedroom.

It was a family room, with one double bed and one single. They sat down on the double one. Charles's hand stroked the so-familiar contours of his wife's shoulders.

"This is another of your detective things, isn't it, Charles?"

He nodded. "Yes. Tomorrow will, I hope, be a significant day."

"Dangerous?"

He shrugged. "I suppose it might be. I hadn't thought. Or it might just be nothing. Me barking up yet another wrong tree."

Frances took his hand. "I wish you wouldn't do it, Charles. I do worry about you, you know."

He felt closer to her than he had for years, as he tried to explain. "It's strange. When something like a murder happens, I just feel I have to sort out what really happened. I feel . . ." he struggled for the right word " . . . responsible."

Frances laughed wryly. "Responsible for anonymous corpses, but when it comes to those close to you . . ."

He felt suitably chastened. "I'm sorry, Frances." He looked out of the window at the clear night over Exmoor. "I was thinking about that today over lunch. About you and me, about . . . you know, responsibility."

"Oh yes?" It wasn't quite cynical, but nearly.

"And whether responsibility and truth are compatible. I've always found truth a problem. That's really why I left you."

"I thought you left me for other women."

"In a way. But it was because I needed other women, and I needed to be truthful about it. I hated all the subterfuges, I hated lying to you. At the time it seemed more truthful to make a break; then at least the position was defined. If I had left you, then I wasn't expected to be . . ."

"Responsible?" Frances supplied.

"I suppose so."

After London, the quiet of the country was almost tangible.

"You know, Frances, I often wonder if we could get back together."

"So do I, Charles." She sighed. "But if it did happen, there are certain things I would demand . . ."

"You could have truth. I've always tried to be truthful to you, Frances."

"And what about that other recurrent word . . . responsible?"

"Hmm."

"There's still the matter of other women."

"Oh, there aren't many of those now. Never have really been many who counted."

"No?"

"No." He sighed. "Hasn't been anyone for months, really, Frances. I don't seem to feel the same urge to wander that I used to."

"All right, Charles," asked Frances softly, "when was the last one?"

Oh dear. He had genuinely forgotten about Dottie Banks until that moment.

And he had promised Frances that he would always be truthful.

"Well, last night, actually. But she didn't mean anything."

Charles spent the night in the single bed.

CHAPTER FIFTEEN

IT MUST have taken a while from Taunton, Charles thought, as Frances drove them in the yellow Renault 5 along the route Lesley-Jane had described. How they ever found time to get there during Peter Hickton's intensive rehearsals, he could not imagine.

But then he remembered that Lesley-Jane and Alex had both been in the company before work on *The Hooded Owl* began. Perhaps they had discovered and used their secret love-nest during the lazier days of the summer.

He glanced sideways at Frances. He thought it might be some time before he was looking for a love-nest again with her. His wife's face was rigidly set, not with anger, which would have been easier to manage, but with hurt, which was almost impossible.

Damn Dottie Banks. And damn all the other Dottie Bankses in his life—all the quick irrelevant lays, who had a nasty habit of suddenly becoming relevant when he was with Frances.

Still, Dottie Banks had given him more than most of the others. She had sent him on the way to solving the mystery of her husband's murder.

"Not far along here," he said. "The North Molton road out of Withypool."

"What are you expecting to find, Charles?"

"I don't know. I just hope it isn't another corpse."

They drew up beside the stone-pillared farm gate which Lesley-Jane had described. Charles got out of the car. It was very muddy underfoot. Damn, he didn't have any boots. Hardly surprising. He hadn't expected a trip down to his daughter's for lunch to end up in the middle of Exmoor.

"Do I come too?" asked Frances. She looked a little less resentful than earlier, and—dare he hope it?—even slightly anxious for him.

"No, love. Stay in the car, if you don't mind."

"All right. I have a book."

"What are you reading?"

"*Rereading Anna Karenina.*"

"Oh well, that should keep you going for a little while."

"You bet."

"Funny, I find I'm rereading more books now. Going through my old favourites. Must be entering the last lap."

"Don't be morbid, Charles."

"No." He outlined a tussock with the toe of his shoe. Now he was so close to a possible solution, he felt the urge to linger. It wasn't exactly that he was afraid; he just didn't want to leave Frances.

"Off you go then."

"Yes. Yes . . ." He turned away and started trudging through the wet grass in the direction Lesley-Jane had specified.

The landscape was very empty. Charles could see why it had appealed to Alex Household. Humankind and human structures seemed a long way away. The hills rolled and folded into each other, hiding little patches of dead ground. The tall, tough grass that covered them ruffled and flattened with the wind, like a cat's fur being stroked. Disgruntled sheep with strange dye markings cropped away at the grass, glowering at Charles as he passed. Anyone who wanted to feel at one with the earth, to shed the twentieth century and all its trappings, might think that here he had achieved his ambition.

No doubt in the summer, the area would be spotted with ardently rucksacked walkers, but it was now early November, and the recent rain and cold would have deterred all but the most perverse. Given shelter, someone might pass undetected in this landscape for some time.

But he'd need a lot of shelter to survive. The cold wind scoured Charles's face and whipped his sodden trousers against his legs. He wished he had brought his overcoat.

He looked round, but the undulations seemed to have shifted, rolled into a new formation. He could not see the distinctive yellow of Frances's car. Still, there was a little stream just beyond the mound to his left. That would give him his bearings again.

He reached the top of the mound and looked down. The stream, like the hills, had moved. He now had no idea where he was.

He looked at his watch. Eleven-twenty. He had to be at the Variety Theatre in Macklin Street at seven-thirty that night for another performance of *The Hooded Owl*. If he wasn't there, he rather feared Paul Lexington might have come to the end of his understudies.

The sky was dull, with a foreboding of rain. He set off briskly in what might be the right direction, but found it difficult to get up any speed over the snagging grass.

He changed his mind, and set off in another right direction, but this offered only more hills. Over each new brow, more hills.

He tried another way, now slightly sweating from anxiety. He didn't care what he found, the car, the stream, or the hut that was the purpose of his visit. Anything that would give him his bearings again. He listened out for the trickle of water, but the wind offered nothing but rustling grass, now very loud in his ears.

Another hill-top gave on to more hills. He turned randomly at right angles, and set off at a lolloping run. His foot caught in the grass, and he sprawled headlong.

He picked himself up and breasted another mound.

Thank God. In the crease of the hills beneath him, in a channel of rushes dark like body-hair against the brightness of the grass, was the stream.

And at the bottom of the dip stood a small stone hut with a broken-backed roof.

He followed the stream down towards it. Presumably once the building had been a shepherd's hut, even his home perhaps, but it was long derelict. The thatch of what remained of the subsided roof was streaked with the dark green of lichen.

It was a dank and unwholesome spot.

And yet he could see how different it must have looked in the summer, how it would have appealed to Alex at the beginning of his supposed new start, and to Lesley-Jane in the throes of her first grown-up affair. It had what all lovers seek, secrecy, privacy, exclusivity. Charles could picture the smugness with which Alex Household would have sat in such a sanctuary and discussed the frenetic activities of the Taunton company. It was a place that offered a kind of peace.

Along the stream pale grey rocks stood exposed. Charles picked his way between them, sometimes having to clamber up, sometimes jumping from one to the other across the water.

As he drew close to the hut, a sense of dread took hold of him. Down

140

in this hollow the sky seemed darker, the wind colder. A fine rain was now dashing against his face.

He felt he was about to find something.

And he feared it would be his friend's body.

"Alex! Alex!" he cried out, not knowing what reply he expected.

He certainly did not expect the shock of a gunshot, cutting through the sounds of the grass.

Nor the sharp impact of the bullet that shattered into the rock a yard in front of him.

Nor the fierce pain in the shin that took his leg from under him and sent him sprawling to the ground.

CHAPTER SIXTEEN

CHARLES FELT the blood trickling down his leg into his wet sock and, still keeping low behind a rock, rolled round to look at the wound.

It was a deep graze, but nothing more. He had been hit, not by the bullet, but by a sliver of quartzy rock. He would undoubtedly survive.

He lay there and thought. If Paul Lexington were describing the situation, he would undoubtedly have said that he had some good news and some bad news. The good news was that Charles's conjecture must have been correct: Alex must be in the hut. The bad news was that Alex had a gun and was shooting at him.

Charles raised his head above the line of the rock and looked down towards the hut. Immediately another shot cracked from the doorway and ricochetted off a rock a couple of yards to his right.

He ducked back.

But after a moment's thought he popped his head up again. It was immediately answered by another shot, which hit a rock behind him.

He lay back down and squinted round. There weren't that many rocks. Certainly not enough to afford shelter for him to get nearer the hut.

But he read another significance into their scarcity. Alex had fired three shots at him from about twenty yards. Each one had missed by at least a yard. But each one had actually hit one of the few rocks scattered around.

Surely that wasn't just bad shooting. A bad shot would have sprayed bullets all over the place, hitting rocks or earth at random. Only someone who was after the maximum deterrent effect would have ensured that each shot hit a rock and caused that terrible screech of ricochet.

In other words, Alex was not shooting to hit him.

Well, it was a theory.

And Charles didn't have many others. From where he was lying, he could neither go forwards nor backwards without exposing himself as a target. So, unless he planned to lie there until nightfall, which would rule out any possibility of his getting up to town to give his evening's performance, he had to make a move.

Besides, his whole thesis, the whole reason why he was there was that he didn't believe Alex Household capable of actually shooting anyone.

He stood up.

A bullet hit a rock three yards in front of him. Confirming his theory.

"Alex, I'm coming down." He stepped forward.

It seemed a long, long walk.

But only one more bullet was fired.

It screamed away from a rock behind him.

When he finally reached the doorway of the hut, he could see Alex Household slumped against it, the arm holding the gun limp at his side.

Had he not known who to expect, he would not have recognised his friend. Through its beard and filth, the face was sunken and ghastly. The eyes flickered feverishly like guttering candles. From the hut came the nauseating stench of human excrement.

"Alex."

"Charles, you shouldn't have come." Alex Household shivered and the words tumbled out unevenly.

"I'm your friend."

"J-j-j-judas was a friend," the filthy skeleton managed to say. "Why not just let me take my chance? If the police find me, that's one thing. But for you to make the trip just to turn me in . . ."

"I haven't come to turn you in."

"Of course you have. Don't pretend. You all think I'm a murderer." The old light of paranoia showed in the feverish eyes.

"No," said Charles. "I know that you didn't shoot Michael Banks."

"What?" Alex Household's body suddenly sagged. He slipped down the door-post to the ground. When Charles knelt to support him, he saw tears in the sick man's eyes.

"You're ill, Alex."

The shaggy head nodded, and then was shaken by a burst of vomiting.

"When did you last eat?"

"I'd left some stuff here. From the summer. Tins and . . . With the gun, too. This place was always my last line of defence, when they . . . when they came to get me . . ." Again the paranoia gleamed. "But I

143

finished all the food . . . I don't know, two days ago, three. Of course, I still had water from the stream, and then . . . the earth's plenty . . ." He gestured feebly around at the hillside.

"You mean grass and . . . ?"

Alex nodded. "Yes, but it . . ." He made a noise that might have been a giggle in happier circumstances " . . . made me ill. Ill." He retched again.

"I must get you to a doctor. Quickly."

Alex shook his head. "No, Charles, please. Just let me die here. It's easier."

"What do you mean?"

"I can't spend my life in some prison. If I'm alive, I need to be free."

"But you will be."

"No, Charles. Everyone thinks I killed Micky Banks. Go on, be truthful. They do, don't they?"

He couldn't help admitting it. "But I know you didn't, Alex."

"Clever old you." This was accompanied by the weakest of smiles. "What do you think happened then?"

"I'll tell you. Stop me when I'm wrong."

"Oh, I will, Charles. I will."

"This is what I think happened that night. I'll grant you were in a bad state, which was hardly surprising after all the business with losing your part and then Lesley-Jane going off with Micky—incidentally, there was less in that than you thought, but that's by the way. O.K., so you had all the motives, you even had the gun, but you didn't do it.

"The gun stayed in the pocket of your jacket in the Green Room until well into the second act. It was taken from there by the murderer, while you were still in the wings, in your shirt-sleeves, feeding Micky his lines through the deaf-aid. The murderer came into the wings with the gun and with the firm intention of shooting someone.

"But this is the bit that took me longest to work out. It's been screaming at me for days, but I just couldn't see it.

"The murderer had no intention of shooting Micky Banks. You were the target.

"When you saw the gun pointing at you, you realised the murderer's intention and begged for mercy. *You* said, 'Oh Lord! No. No, put it down. You mustn't do that to me. You daren't. Please. Please . . .' I should have realised that from the fact that Micky said 'Oh Lord'—an expression, incidentally, that wasn't in the script of the play and that he had never used in his life—*before* he turned round from the Hooded Owl

144

and looked into the wings. So it wasn't a reaction from him. He was merely relaying what he heard over his deaf-aid.

"I should have realised it earlier. I've been working with the deaf-aid for over a week, for God's sake, and I realised how much I rely on it. When you're using it, you just repeat the words you hear, regardless of the sense. I got caught last week because I got fed the wrong line. Even if it's nonsense, you still repeat it.

"Which is what Micky Banks did. He just kept repeating what you were saying. He knew there was something odd, which was why he turned round to look into the wings, hoping for some signal from you.

"By then I reckon you had your back to the stage and were facing the barrel of the gun. At the moment the murderer squeezed the trigger, you threw yourself sideways, the bullet missed you, but hit Micky Banks, who was standing directly behind you.

"You then looked round in shock to see him fall. At that moment Lesley-Jane saw your face—she told me you 'looked over your shoulder at her', but I didn't at the time realise that meant you must have been facing away from the stage. Anyway, Lesley-Jane jumped to the conclusion that everyone else has since jumped to—that you shot Micky—and screamed.

"The murderer was meanwhile standing, shocked at what had happened, but still holding the gun. Rather than risk the danger of another shot, you followed your natural instinct to run. You grabbed your jacket from the Green Room and rushed out of the theatre.

"It was probably only when you got outside that you realised how much circumstances looked against you. All your recurrent fears of the world ganging up on you came to the surface, and you ran away. Somehow you got down here, where you have been since, quietly starving and poisoning yourself to death.

"After you had gone, the murderer went backstage, abandoning the gun on the way. The hue and cry started for you, but you could not be found. Rumours spread that you had committed suicide. This was all good news for the murderer. So long as you didn't reappear, or if, when you did reappear, you were dead, there was no danger of the police looking for any other killer.

"The accidental shooting of Michael Banks must have been a shock, but, as time passed, the murderer must have begun to feel very secure from the danger of discovery."

Charles looked at Alex's haggard face, which now glowed with a new light. "How'm I doing so far?"

145

"Bloody marvellous, Charles. That's exactly what happened." A shadow passed over his face. "But how you're ever going to convince anyone else that's what happened, I don't know . . ."

"If we explain to the police . . ."

Alex shook his head. "Come on, Charles. The police are not notorious for their imagination. Everything is stacked against me, you have to admit. I bet the gun was even covered in my fingerprints."

Charles had to admit that it was.

"So *I* know. And now, thanks to a very neat bit of deduction, *you* know. But I don't see that either of us could produce a shred of evidence to support our extremely unlikely thesis, so I don't see that we're much further advanced. If I give myself up, I'll be charged with murder."

"Hmm," said Charles. "Then what I'll have to do is to get a confession from the real murderer."

Alex snorted hopelessly. "Good luck."

"I think it may be possible. And that, of course," said Charles, "brings me to the identity of the real murderer.

"Very difficult to work that out at first. So long as I was looking for someone who might want to murder Michael Banks, I was getting nowhere. But once I got the right victim, finding the right murderer became easier."

"Who do you think it was then?" asked Alex.

Charles told him.

"Dead right," said Alex.

Charles looked a mess when he got back to the car, but Frances made no comment. Nor did she mention the fact that she'd been sitting there for nearly three hours.

"How's *Anna Karenina*?"

"Fine. She is now living with Vronsky as if they were married."

"Good for her. Mind you, it'll end in tears."

"And how are you?"

"Fine."

"Anything I can do for you?"

"There are three things, actually."

"Name them and I'll see if I can help."

"Right. First, I would like you to drive me to Taunton, so that I can catch a train back to London, in order to be at the Variety Theatre this evening for—among other things—a performance of *The Hooded Owl*."

"That's possible."

"Second, I want you to buy blankets, food, a portable heater and some sort of stomach medicine, and come back here . . ."

"Right here?"

"Yes. Then I want you to follow instructions I will give you to a small derelict hut, where you will find a very sick man, who needs looking after . . ."

"Shouldn't I get a doctor too?"

"No. Not for the moment. I promised him I wouldn't involve anyone official until I've . . . sorted something out for him."

"And how long am I likely to have to play Florence Nightingale? When will you have sorted this something out for him?"

"I'll do it tonight. Then I'll let the emergency services know and someone will come out for him."

"I see. Well, that sounds a jolly way to spend a half-term. And, if I may ask, what was the third thing?"

"To give me another chance."

"Oh, Charles," said Frances sadly, "I'm not so sure about that."

CHAPTER SEVENTEEN

THE TRAIN from Taunton was delayed. It was after the "half" when Charles arrived at the Variety Theatre. The business of getting into costume and make-up and then giving his performance as the father in Malcolm Harris's *The Hooded Owl* meant that details like confrontations with murderers would have to wait.

He was on stage for most of the first act, and it was only when the curtain fell for the interval that he could concentrate on anything other than the play.

As soon as he walked into the Green Room, he knew that something was wrong. Actors and actresses, who spend all their professional lives creating fictional atmospheres, do not stint themselves when real opportunities come along.

"What's up?" he asked Salome Search, who was draped over a sofa doing Mrs. Siddons impressions.

"It's Lesley-Jane," the actress breathed dramatically.

"What? What's happened to her?"

"She passed out in the wings after her last exit."

"Good God!"

"Yes, she was in a dead faint."

"Where is she?"

"She's been taken up to her dressing room. The St. John Ambulance man's up there with her."

"Do you know what it is?"

"No. But . . ." Salome Search's three years at R.A.D.A. had taught her that the pause before a sensational line can be extended almost infinitely. "There was blood in the wings."

"Oh, my God!" Charles turned towards the Green Room door and the stairs to the dressing rooms.

But the doorway was blocked by the figure of Wallas Ward, holding up limp hands for attention.

"Ladies and gentlemen," said the Company Manager, "you may

148

already have heard that Miss Decker was taken ill at the end of the first act. It seems that she will not be well enough to proceed with the rest of the play, and so her understudy will be taking over the role. Now it's not going to be easy for the girl, so I hope you will give her all the support you can. I will be making an announcement to the audience before the curtain rises."

"Is she all right?" asked Charles desperately.

"Yes, she's fine. Just weak. We've rung for her mother who's going to come and take her home. The St. John Ambulance man doesn't reckon she needs to go to the hospital."

"What's wrong with her? Do you know?"

The Company Manager looked embarrassed. "Women's things," he said with distaste.

"Is she on her own up there?"

"No, the St. John Ambulance man's still there. And Paul went to see what was up. Oh, and I think Malcolm Harris was one of the ones who helped her up. He may still be up there. So she's got plenty of people."

"I think I'd better go up and see her."

But before he could, the Company Manager stopped him with an admonitory "Incidentally, Mr. Paris . . ."

"Yes?"

"I gather you were late for the 'half' tonight."

"Yes. I was in a train that got delayed."

"Where were you coming from?"

"Taunton."

Wallas Ward tutted, spinster-like. "Mr. Paris, you should have left more time. While you are contracted for a West End show, it is very irresponsible to go such a long way. In fact, I wouldn't be surprised if there were a clause in your contract forbidding that kind of journey on a performance day. Remember, you are under contract to Scenario Productions and—"

"I thought I was under contract to Paul Lexington Productions."

"No, Paul is now working through a new company."

"Why?"

"That is not at the moment relevant," reprimanded the Company Manager. "I am talking about your lateness for the 'half'."

"Yes, all right. Well, I'm very sorry. Won't do it again. Now if you'd—"

"And another thing," Wallas Ward continued inexorably. "The lines in the first act were very sloppy this evening. I had a note from Malcolm

Harris who was out front and was very annoyed about it. You got badly lost in the dinner party scene."

"Yes, that was because Lesley-Jane was giving me the wrong cues. Her lines were all over the place tonight."

"Yes, Malcolm Harris mentioned that, too. Presumably that was because she was unwell. But in your case, when you have every line being repeated in your ear, it's unforgivable."

"But if you get the wrong cues, you have to adjust the lines to make sense of the dialogue."

"That's as maybe, but Malcolm Harris said—"

"Look, come on. Every author is obsessed about his lines. You don't have to—"

"It is my job as Company Manager," said Wallas Ward primly, "to listen to points from everyone in the company and the author is just as important as—"

"I would have thought it was also important for you to keep the author informed of everything that's going on. Do you know, on the first night, Malcolm Harris didn't know about the cuts we'd had to make for time. He thought Micky Banks was just randomly slashing great chunks out of his script."

"I agree. He should have been told. And he was extremely annoyed that evening when he came round at the interval. But I pointed out to him that Mr. Banks was not making cuts himself—he was merely repeating the lines he heard in his earphone."

"And you said that Alex was reading from a cut script?"

"I didn't have time to do that. Mr. Harris rushed off in something of a paddy."

"I've got to get upstairs and see Lesley-Jane!" hissed Charles.

Wallas Ward stepped aside with mock-deference.

But as soon as his foot was on the first step of the stairs, Charles heard the fatal summons over the loudspeaker.

"Beginners, Act Two, please."

He froze. It was rarely that he felt such a direct clash between his twin roles as actor and detective.

But there was no doubt which triumphed. Thirty-two years of professional conditioning left him no alternative.

He turned round and walked towards the stage.

The father was on for the whole of the second act of *The Hooded Owl*, and never had that part of the play passed as slowly as it did that evening.

Mechanically going through the motions, repeating his words, hardly aware of the small Monday night audience, hardly aware of the new girl hesitantly feeding him Lesley-Jane's lines, he was in an agony of apprehension throughout the performance.

But he had to play his part through to the end.

The end of the play, one curtain-call, and then, sod it, he'd risk another slap on the wrist from the arch Mr. Ward. He rushed offstage and up to Lesley-Jane's dressing room.

He tapped on the door and entered.

There were four people inside.

And one of them was Michael Banks's murderer.

Lesley-Jane lay on the daybed in her kimono. She was drained of all colour and animation, but alive.

Her mother, Valerie Cass, was busying herself, packing things into a small overnight case.

Paul Lexington (now of Scenario Productions) was looking at Lesley-Jane anxiously and asking if he should arrange an ambulance.

Malcolm Harris sat disconsolately in a chair, chewing his fingernails.

"No, for the last time, she'll be quite all right," said Valerie Cass, in reply to Paul. She looked round to see Charles. "Oh, not another man. Really. Just leave us alone, will you, all of you? Lesley-Jane's quite all right now I'm here. Only a woman can understand what's wrong, and there's nothing any of you could do. So thank you for your concern, but will you now please go."

"Look, we're worried about her," grumbled Malcolm Harris.

"If you don't want me to call an ambulance, I'll drive her to the hospital, if you like," offered Paul Lexington.

"No, thank you very much. We needn't involve hospitals."

"I think she should be seen by a doctor," the producer insisted. "Look, I'm employing her. I have to know how long she's likely to be out of commission."

"Oh, I should think she'd be all right," said Charles. And then, deciding that it was time to start dropping bombshells, "Some actresses have continued acting well into the eighth month of pregnancy."

He should have realised it before, but it was only when he had seen Juliet that the obvious had appeared in all its blatancy. The same strained paleness. Even the detail of needing a sleep in the afternoon.

Lesley-Jane herself was the only one who didn't react. The two men looked at him open-mouthed. But Valerie Cass's response was the most interesting. She turned to Charles with an almost beatific expression and said, "Well done. Yes, the little secret is out. I am to become a grandmother."

To say "Congratulations" somehow seemed inappropriate. Instead, he asked cautiously, "Even after tonight?"

"Oh yes," replied Valerie with breezy gynaecological certainty. "That was just a little 'show'. Lesley-Jane will be fine if she just rests up for a few days. Exactly the same thing happened to me at the same stage when I was pregnant."

"I . . . um . . . think I'd better be off," said Malcolm Harris awkwardly.

Charles stood aside, and let him go.

Paul Lexington also looked embarrassed. "Well, of course, this will affect her availability for the show."

"As I say, only for a few days. Then she'll be fine. It'll be a good three months before she shows, and, with skilful dressing, she could go on a lot longer."

"But," said Charles, "It's going to curtail her theatrical career a bit, isn't it?"

"Oh no." Valerie Cass looked at him radiantly. "I've got it all worked out. I will be able to look after the baby. Lesley-Jane's career will be hardly interrupted. No, no, my little girl's talent will still take her right to the top."

The prospect realised Valerie Cass's most exotic dreams. Her daughter would be perpetually in her debt, perpetually chained to her, and she would have the new stimulus of another baby to bring up. Best of all, there would be no father around to challenge her supremacy over either her child or her grandchild.

"Hmm," grunted Paul Lexington. "I still think she should see a doctor."

"I'll get our family doctor to take a look at her in the morning. There—will that satisfy you?"

"I suppose it'll have to. Let me know what the prospects are."

"I will."

Paul Lexington moved towards the door.

Charles stood aside, and let him go.

"Well, now, Charles. As you see, everything is fine. I'm now going to take my little baby home. So there's nothing to keep you here."

"Oh, but there is," said Charles. "I want to talk about Alex Household."

152

"I can't think what relevance he has to anything."

"Can't you? He's the child's father."

"As I say, I can't think what relevance he has to anything." In those words Valerie Cass expressed everything she felt about the relationship between the sexes.

"You think the father is irrelevant?"

"Yes. It's the woman who carries the child, the woman who does the work, the man does nothing."

Charles restrained his anger, and started on a new tack. "It was on the first night that Lesley-Jane told you she was pregnant."

Valerie Cass was silent, surprised by the change of direction.

"She told you Alex was the father, and suddenly you saw the awful vision of history repeating itself. You saw Lesley-Jane's career being cut short by pregnancy, just as yours had been. And all your hatred of men, all the anger you have used to make your own husband's life a misery, it all became focused on Alex Household. Not only did he threaten your daughter's career, he also threatened to take her away from you."

Valerie Cass now looked as pale as her daughter. "I don't know what you're talking about."

"I'm talking about the death of Michael Banks. I'm talking about the taking of human life. I'm talking about murder."

There was a wail from the bed and, for the first time since Charles had entered the room, Lesley-Jane spoke. "I have taken human life," she cried. "I am the murderer!"

They both looked at her in amazement. Tears were running freely down the girl's face. She clutched at herself to claw away a sudden pain.

Charles understood. He hadn't known until that moment, but now he understood. "But the life you have taken," he said gently, "was not that of Michael Banks. Was it?"

The girl shook her head tearfully.

"No, the life you have taken is the life of your baby. You had an abortion today, didn't you?"

She nodded.

"Which is why you passed out. Why you are in this state now."

"No!" screamed Valerie Cass. "No, you didn't!"

Lesley-Jane looked at her mother. The tears were receding and there was a hardness in her eyes.

But Valerie refused to believe their message. "It's a woman's sacred duty to bear children. That's what we were put here for."

"Listen, Mummy." Lesley-Jane had control of herself again and spoke evenly. "The child effectively had no father."

"But it would have had you. And me."

"I didn't want it. I got pregnant because you spent all my life filling my head with romantic ideas rather than giving me any practical advice. If I had had the baby, I would never have been able to pick up my career again."

"But as I said, I would have looked after it."

"What?" hissed Lesley-Jane. "And turned it into another confused, neurotic mess like me?"

"But, darling, suppose I had done the same when I was expecting you? Suppose I had had an abortion?"

Lesley-Jane looked at her mother without any trace of affection. "It would have been the best thing you could ever have done for me. Someone like you is not qualified to bring up children."

Valerie Cass sank back into a chair as if she had been slapped. There was no resistance left in her, just a void of pain.

Charles said what he had to say, softly but firmly.

"What you did after you heard about your daughter's pregnancy was hardly rational. You went down towards the stage, vowing revenge on her . . . her what? . . . seducer? You looked for him in the Green Room, but found only his jacket. In its pocket you found the gun.

"You went into the wings on the O.P. side of the stage to shoot Alex Household. He saw you coming and begged for mercy, not realising that his words were being transmitted and repeated by Michael Banks on stage. At the moment you fired the gun, Alex dodged, and Michael was killed.

"Alex rushed off. You left the stage, abandoning the gun as you went. Then I should think you came up here, and that was probably the first time you realised what had happened. Also the first time you realised how unlikely your crime was ever to be discovered. No one had seen you, you were wearing gloves so there were no fingerprints on the gun, and Alex Household's flight looked like an admission of guilt.

"If he had never been found, you'd have got away with it. But I spoke to Alex today, and he confirmed what I've just described to you."

"He's alive?" asked Lesley-Jane softly.

"Yes, he's alive."

There was a long silence. Then Valerie Cass looked at Charles. There was a new glow of resolution in her eyes, and he feared she was about to deny everything. If she did, he didn't know what he would do; he had not a shred of evidence.

But no.

"Very well," she announced. "I admit it. I killed Michael Banks."

She spoke boldly, like Charlotte Corday, like Joan of Arc. Charles understood what had caused her new surge of spirit.

Valerie Cass had found a new role to play. It was the one she had been rehearsing for all her life—that of martyr.

CHAPTER EIGHTEEN

DURING THE ensuing week, *The Hooded Owl* seemed to be gaining momentum. The audiences were growing almost imperceptibly, and the word-of-mouth was good. One or two of the national papers, feeling guilty about the show's first night, sent second-string critics along for a second look, and their reports were, on the whole, favourable.

The performances gained in strength. On the Thursday, Lesley-Jane Decker came back into the cast. After the abortion and her mother's arrest, she seemed to have matured. She approached her work with a new single-mindedness, and acted better than ever.

Charles Paris got better, too. On the Tuesday night, as an experiment, without telling anyone (least of all Wallas Ward), he had a word with the A.S.M. before the show, and asked him not to feed the lines until absolutely necessary. To Charles's amazement, he managed to get through the whole show without a single prompt. The constant repetition had fixed the lines indelibly in his mind.

The loss of this crutch did not, as he had feared, diminish his confidence. Instead, it made him feel more relaxed, stronger, more in control. And he knew this improvement was reflected in his acting.

He also came to rely less on drink. He had proved he could give a performance without it, and, though it frightened him to remove another support, he dared another night without his customary stimulus. To his surprise, he found his head was clearer, his concentration better, and his nerves no worse. He repeated the experiment on subsequent nights, and felt better for it. He'd still wind down with a couple of large Bell's, but he got out of the habit of drinking before the show.

He also spoke to his agent, and the company Equity representative, and finally to Paul Lexington direct, about his unsatisfactory status in the play, acting the part regularly and being paid only as an understudy. The producer, probably already under pressure from Equity, and

156

unwilling to take on the expense of another star, agreed that he would regularise the position as soon as possible.

So, for a couple of weeks, *The Hooded Owl* soldiered on in the West End. Everyone knew the early weeks would be tense. Like a sick baby, a show has to be carefully nursed until it can build up its own strength.

But *The Hooded Owl* seemed to be winning the fight for survival. The audiences in the second week after Valerie Cass's arrest were definitely getting bigger, and their reaction more positively approving. At this rate, the production should soon reach the break-even point its budget required.

A few coach parties started to come. Soon the show would be an established signpost in the Entertainments columns of the newspapers, and begin to run on its own momentum.

When the company was summoned to a meeting on stage at the "half" on the Friday of that week, they expected some sort of announcement of how near they were to their break-even. The signs were good. They had been running for nearly a month and were gaining strength daily.

They were in for a disappointment.

Wallas Ward clapped his limp hands for silence, and began without Paul Lexington's ambivalent opening.

"Ladies and gentlemen, I am afraid I have some bad news.

"As you know, today is the day you should be paid. Since the money goes to your agents in most cases, you won't yet have noticed anything wrong. But I'm afraid I have to tell you that no money has been sent to your agents."

He raised his hands again to still the outcry which this provoked.

"Ladies and gentlemen, I am sorry, but it appears that there is no money anywhere in this show. The production company has gone bankrupt."

The screams of fury which greeted this finally resolved themselves into one question: Where was Paul Lexington?

"I am sorry, ladies and gentlemen, but I cannot answer that. Not for any reason of discretion or protecting him; the fact is, I do not know where Paul Lexington is. He hasn't been seen round the theatre for two days and, when I spoke to his landlord this afternoon, I discovered that he had left his flat yesterday, taking all his belongings and owing three months' rent."

In fact, not to put too fine a point on it, Paul Lexington had done a bunk. Living up to another stereotype of the theatrical producer, though

157

not usually the sort of producer who reached the heights of the West End.

So that was it.

"As a result, ladies and gentlemen," the Company Manager concluded unctuously, "I regret to inform you that the notices will go up tonight. We will do the two performances tomorrow, because of advance bookings, but I'm afraid otherwise, that is the end."

So it was that, after three and a half weeks at the Variety Theatre, *The Hooded Owl* by Malcolm Harris closed.

"Could I speak to Gerald Venables, please? It's Charles Paris speaking."

"I'll put you through."

"Charles! Sorry to hear about the show. I'm afraid that Paul Lexington was a bad lot."

"To put it mildly."

"Indeed. As you know, I'm trying to sort out Bobby Anscombe's end, and it's only now I'm beginning to see the full extent of the mess. Lexington owed money everywhere. God knows how he got as far as he did. So far as I can see, once Bobby was out, he was running the production on sheer cheek."

"That was one thing he didn't lack."

"No. He seems to have kept going for a while by constantly starting up new companies and borrowing on them, but quite honestly it's going to be some time before everything's crawled out of the woodwork and I can get a clear picture."

"What'll happen to him?"

"I don't know. I doubt if he'll get prosecuted unless one of his creditors decides to make the effort. He hasn't got any assets—apart from the fact that he's vanished off the face of the earth—so there's not a lot of point in suing him. That's what I'm going to advise Bobby."

"He seemed so plausible."

"Of course he did. To all of you in the company. He always said what you wanted to hear. He painted in your dreams for you."

"Yes."

"Trouble is, he was really out of his league. Trying to tangle with the big boys like Bobby. And Denis Thornton was ripping him off, too."

"Was he?"

"Oh yes. Lanthorn Productions only took on the show because they didn't want the Variety Theatre dark."

"Really?"

"Yes. They just wanted a show in there, because they'd acquired the lease and wanted to demonstrate that it could still work as a theatre."

"But I thought *The Hooded Owl* was going to be their big opening."

"No, no. That's going to be a revival of *Flower Drum Song* in March. Been planned for months."

"But if *The Hooded Owl* had run, we'd still have been there in March."

"Denis Thornton knew it wouldn't run. He's a wily old bird. Best thing that happened for him when Paul agreed to let Show-Off do the publicity. Since they're part of Lanthorn, Denis could control how much coverage your show got."

"You mean he deliberately limited our publicity?"

"Ooh, mustn't say that. Might be slander. Let's just say that most of Show-Off's energies during the week of your opening went into Lanthorn Productions' new musical at the King's."

"But surely that's criminal?"

"Tut, tut, you mustn't use words like that, Charles. When you've been dealing with theatre managements as long as I have, you come to realise that there's a very thin dividing line between skilful dealing and what you choose to call crime. Paul Lexington wasn't sufficiently experienced, so he ended up the wrong side of that line."

"Hmm. I wonder what'll happen to him."

"Well, I think it'll be a long time before he surfaces in the West End again. The Society of West End Theatre Managers'll see to that."

"Yes, but I've somehow a feeling he'll pop up again somewhere. That sort always finds someone new to believe them."

"True. Incidentally, Charles, Kate was saying the other day what a long time it is since we've seen you, and wouldn't it be nice if you could come over for dinner one of these evenings. I said it'd be difficult because you'd got the show, but now of course . . ."

"Yes. Sounds great."

"With Frances, of course. I mean, I gathered at that first night that you were back together again. You are, aren't you?"

"Well . . . er . . . not exactly."

So what happened to them all in the weeks running up to Christmas?

Valerie Cass was convicted of killing Michael Banks, but the charge, to which she readily confessed, was manslaughter, and she was sentenced to three years in prison.

Lesley-Jane Decker landed a very good part in a television series about the Bloomsbury Group, which guaranteed her six months' work and national recognition when the show hit the screens. She also, in her mother's absence, got to know her father for the first time, and found she got on with him very well.

Alex Household spent two weeks in hospital and, when he came out, decided to give up acting and join a monastery dedicated to a pantheistic view of the universe.

Peter Hickton kept his cast up most nights rehearsing for the Prince's Theatre, Taunton's annual pantomime, *Babes in the Wood*, in which Salome Search played a somewhat gnarled principal boy.

Paul Lexington, from his new base in Hull, set up a company called Pierre Productions, whose aim was to put Northern club comics into end-of-the-pier summer seasons.

Malcolm Harris, who had received no money from the production of *The Hooded Owl* except for the pittance of the long-lapsed option, went back to his schoolteaching. In his evenings he worked on a play about Mary, Queen of Scots, because his wife's mother had read somewhere that costume drama was coming back.

Dottie Banks continued to entertain a stream of men in Hans Crescent. Then, to everyone's surprise, she died of a drug overdose on Christmas Eve. She must have missed her husband more than she showed.

George Birkitt received the first scripts for a new series of *Fly-Buttons* and sent them back to the producer, complaining that his character hadn't got enough lines. He also opened two super-markets, which pleased him greatly, suggesting as it did that people were starting to think of him as a star.

Wallas Ward met a very nice black dancer at a party and settled down with him in Pimlico.

Frances Paris had an offer on the house in Muswell Hill. It was two thousand less than the asking price, but, because the housing market was depressed, and on the advice of her son-in-law, she accepted it.

And Charles Paris? He got drunk.